T.L. Burrell ✠ Racheal Gauley

Eathair

Lulu Enterprises Inc.

Raleigh

This book is a work of fiction. Any references to historical events, real people, or real locales are used fictitiously. Other names, characters, places, and incidents are the product of the author's imagination, and any resemblance to actual events or locales or persons, living or dead, is entirely coincidental.

Lulu Enterprises, Inc.

3101 Hillsborough Street, Raleigh, NC 27607

Printed by Lulu Press, Raleigh, NC

Published by T.L. Burrell & Racheal Gauley

The text of this book was set in Calibri and Times New Roman.

10 9 8 7 6 5 4 3 2 1

ISBN-13: 978-1-329-19908-8

Printed in the U.S.A.

"I would like to thank my sister, Racheal, for all the work she has put into this book and for always being there for me and encouraging me to keep writing. I would also like to thank my readers for buying, but more importantly, reading this book."

~ ***T.L. Burrell***

"Thank you so much to everyone who has encouraged us with praise and support! Even if it's from only a few people, it's that little bit of encouragement that keeps me going, and I hope to live up to the expectations of giving my sister and our fans a quality piece of literature they can enjoy."

~ ***Racheal G.***

Raiden & Avani by Dakota Green

Table of Contents

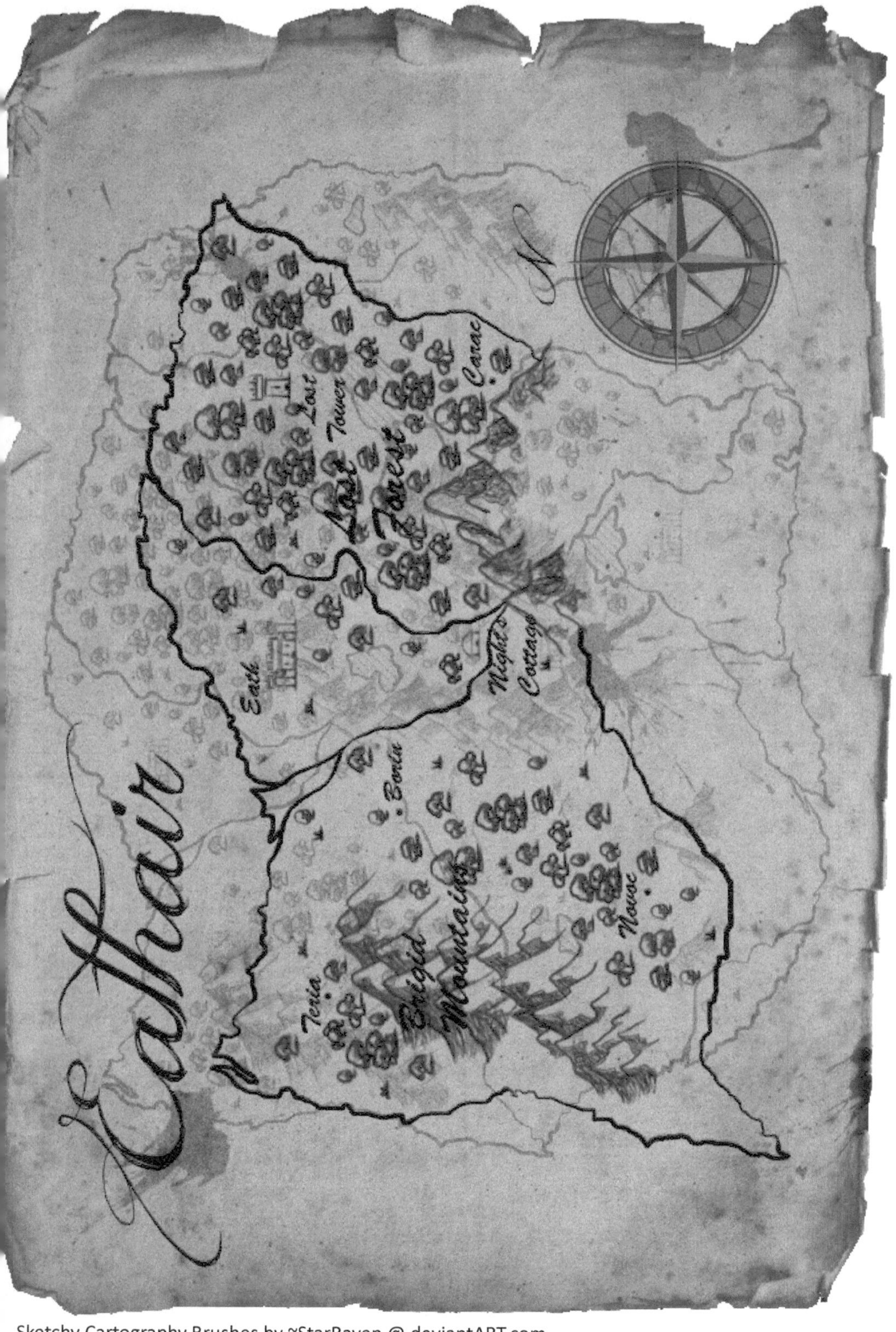

Sketchy Cartography Brushes by ~StarRaven @ deviantART.com
old paper stock 02 by =ftourini @ deviantART.com
Compass Rose by ~Sarrel @ deviantART.com

Prologue

"Sorry Rachael isn't here to join us, Seth." Leon said as he sat on a table in Seth's office.

"She's with Besky working to rebuild Nymphen right?" Seth asked. Leon nodded and then turned his injured arm to Seth, being careful not to stretch it past its limits.

"So what did you do?" Seth said as he examined Leon's arm. It was bruised heavily as if he had been grabbed by a large hand. Touching it lightly, Seth sighed at the hiss of pain Leon let loose. The arm was broken.

"Well I was teaching Revy and Savannah the Ancient Language when Revy used the wrong word. I was trying to teach them how to heal, but instead Revy summoned a monster and...my arm kind of got in the way." Leon said, a small smile on his face. He loved his family and he loved to teach his children all he could about magic.

Seth chuckled and then set to work grabbing some splints and making Leon wince as he pulled the bandage tight around his arm.

"That should take care of it. Now, drink this to reduce the pain, but be careful as it may make you drowsy. I have one question for you though: Why didn't you heal yourself?"

Leon gulped then took the medicine.

"Thanks Seth, and well Ancient Magic is not something you can just snap your fingers and heal, and Rachael wasn't here to heal me. Anyway thanks for taking the time to see me, I know you want to be with Skyla and your little ones." Leon said with a teasing tone.

"Ah, but you forget about my sister-in-law being here with her little *monster*. That boy has taken his mother's magic to the next level—you never know who he is or where he is." Seth replied with a smirk.

"I bet Dimitreith is having trouble keeping up with that little one if he's that advanced already."

Seth chuckled at the statement.

"Yes he is. Well don't hesitate to come see me the next time you're in Clydia, and bring Rachael and the kids too! It would be nice to see them again."

Leon nodded as he left, happy to be going home to Rachael and his children with plans of how to improve his teaching so another incident like this would not happen again.

Half way from the inn Leon began stumbling over his own feet, the medicine taking effect, making him decide to stay another night at an inn and then teleport home the next day. Leon was walking through a dark alley almost to the inn when he was grabbed from behind and a cold familiar voice whispered into his ear,

"Good to see you again, Leon. Did you miss me?"

After these words were said Leon only had time to register that he was being taken away before all went black.

Chapter One

A boy sat in a window looking out over the vast array of trees that made up the forests of Eathair.

"Raiden, have you seen Lady Avani?" a tall slender girl asked the boy as she brushed imaginary dirt from her maid skirt. The boy raised his head, his metallic blue eyes piercing into the girl's green.

"No I haven't." he answered. The girl nodded and then turned and left to do the rest of her chores, seemingly unworried about her wayward mistress. After she left Raiden turned to the widow, his gaze coming to rest on the forest looming in the distance and a worried expression on his face.

"Avani, where are you?"

The leaves swayed in the trees as the wind passed through them and the birds sang their melodies lazily in the heat of the afternoon. Sitting under a tree Avani looked up from her map, knowing she would have to go home soon. Smirking, Avani stood. If her mother knew she was out wandering in the Lost Woods she would never be allowed to leave the castle again. *Forests were no place for a lady*, her mother would say, but Avani felt connected to the forest—it called her, and she enjoyed the peace it would bring to her mind whenever she visited.

Avani started to walk towards Eath, the capital of Eathair and the prison cell she liked to call home, when a blood-curdling scream broke the calm of the forest, sending a chill down Avani's spine. Soon Avani found herself running toward the source of the sound, both from panic and curiosity, her feet pounding on the solid earth below and the forest seeming to lead the way for her. Then she found herself in front of the Lost Tower, its brick walls crumbling and ivy crawling toward the sky. Another scream sounded and Avani felt it chill her to the bone, but then she let it slide, figuring it was the ghosts who were supposed to live in the tower left over from some war, and began making her way home.

Raiden was just entering the entry way when Avani walked in, her long blonde hair a mess and her clothes covered in grass and dirt stains, and Raiden couldn't have felt more love for her than in that moment as she stooped to brush grass from her pants. She looked up and upon seeing Raiden her amethyst eyes sparkled.

"Oh Raiden, you should have come with me! The forest was so beautiful today! The air just seemed alive and the birds were singing so sweetly..."

Raiden smiled, hiding the love in his heart just barely and then walked over to stand next to Avani, pulling a twig out of her hair.

"So that's what you were doing today? You're lucky your mother didn't notice your absence."

Avani blew her hair out of her face and then smirked.

"As if she would. She's too busy trying to turn my brother into a proper heir, but I should change before she sees me."

Raiden nodded and then watched Avani race up the stairs, a small smile still gracing his lips.

Avani sighed as she examined herself in the mirror. She hated wearing dresses, because they felt so restricting, but her mother would never let her in court if she was wearing pants and that was where all the fun was in the castle. Avani turned and then left her room to find her cousin Terra. She loved hearing tales from when Terra had helped save Watair from Rena.

Entering the throne room, Avani was happy to see Terra wave

her over to the table she was sitting at.

"I heard you went into the forest again." Terra said playfully, "You know, one of these days Auntie is going to notice that you're gone all the time."

Avani smiled and then sat down.

"She's too busy with my older brother to notice me. Besides, you know how much I love the forest."

Terra smiled. She was about to say something when a guard walked up to the table escorting a woman and two children. The woman's light blonde hair stretched to the small of her back and her light blue eyes were filled with emotion. The little girl next to her was twirling a lock of her long red hair around one of her small fingers and her golden eyes were so filled with distress that Avani felt sad. The little boy beside her was calm, his short silver hair slightly messy and his deep blue eyes tranquil.

"My Lady, this woman claims to know you."

The guard's gruff voice made Avani stop her staring and look to her cousin. Terra smiled brightly, her eyes sparkling.

"Yes, I know her."

The guard nodded, his face slightly pinched in anger, and then left. Avani noticed the woman's skin was a pale green as she approached Terra.

"Rachael, it's so nice to see you. What has it been, two years?"

Rachael smiled and nodded, although her smile did not reach her eyes.

"Yes, that seems right. I hope all is well with you?"

Terra nodded, her face a mask of contentment, then she reached her arms out.

"Come here Revy, Savannah. I want a hug."

Revy and Savannah smiled and then rushed into Terra's arms,

giggling.

"So how are you and Leon?" Terra asked as she released the children from her hug. Rachael's small smile vanished and her eyes once again became filled with emotion.

"That's why I'm here...you see, Leon is missing. Last week he went to see Seth about his arm and then he simply never came home. I followed his magic for a short time, but it vanished after I entered Eathair so I know he's here, I just don't know where. Can you help me? You know Eathair much better than I do."

Terra frowned.

"I wish I could, but I'm needed here right now. My father is getting ready to pass the throne to me."

Rachael sighed and then turned to leave, the disappointment leaking from her.

"Wait! I can help you!" Avani said, a gleam in her eyes at the thought of being in an adventure as grand as Terra's was and the freedom the adventure promised. Rachael raised her eyebrow and then looked at Terra in a silent question.

"You know your mother will never allow that." Terra stated. Avani started to say something when a woman's voice asked,

"Never allow what?"

Avani and Terra turned to the voice. A woman stood behind them, her charcoal hair flowed down to the back of her knees and her steel gray eyes were focused completely on Avani's face. Avani stood.

"You would never let me guide Rachael through the kingdom."

The woman shook her head.

"You're right, I would never allow you to go..."

Anger showed on Avani's face and she raised her fists.

"But mother!"

Avani was silenced by a look from her mother.

"Let me finish. I would not allow you to go *alone*. If you want to go, Raiden must go with you."

Avani smiled in both disbelief and happiness then hugged her mother.

"Thank you mom!"

Avani's mother smiled.

"Well it's certainly better than you going into the Lost Woods every day when you think I don't notice you're gone."

Avani blushed then turned to Rachael, beaming.

"Come on, let's get Raiden so we can get going!"

Rachael nodded and then followed Avani out to the stables.

"Raiden has a way with animals so he's always at the stables. The stable master just loves it when Raiden's there."

When they entered the stables, Rachael saw a young man with jaw-length platinum blonde hair that shined dully in the stable's light. He was slightly bent over and whispering something into a colt's ear. However, when he saw Avani the young man stood and smiled.

"What can I do for you, Avani?" he asked, his metallic blue eyes shining. Avani returned the smile.

"Well Raiden I have a favor to ask. You see, Rachael here needs me to guide her around the kingdom so will you please join us?"

Raiden tilted his head to the side as if thinking, but then he nodded. Avani giggled and then turned to Rachael.

"Where to first?"

Rachael smiled.

"I need to see an old friend before we start looking for Leon."

Raiden and Avani nodded.

A short while later they followed Rachael out the castle gates. As they left, a group of small birds flew to Raiden and landed on his shoulders. Raiden chuckled and then whistled and the birds flew off.

"What was that about?" Avani asked. Raiden smiled.

"They just wanted to say good bye."

As the group came to a small cottage nestled within a remote set of trees, a man burst out the front door in a panic, tripping and landing flat on his face. Rachael rushed to the man and helped him up, slight amusement showing on her face.

"Are you okay, Night?"

The man named Night looked up and Avani gasped. Night's eyes were a startling sky blue that stood out from his pale face which was framed by messy black hair.

"I'm fine I think...maybe...I just don't know." Night sighed, his body sagging. Rachael chuckled.

"What's got you so mixed up, Night?"

Night sighed again, sagging farther toward the ground.

"Ninena is going into labor and I have no idea what to do!"

Rachael smiled.

"Watch Revy and Savannah." Rachael ordered. "Avani, you come with me."

Avani smiled at both the nervousness Night displayed and the thought of helping bring a new life into the world and then followed Rachael. Upon opening the door to the cottage, they were both greeted by the sight of a young boy. Looking down, the first thing Avani saw was his messy mop of blonde hair that reached no higher than Revy or Savannah. The boy looked up, his brilliant orange eyes reminiscent of the setting sun, but the rest of his features dull and filled with concern.

"Is...is Ninena going to be okay?" he asked in a hushed tone, his eyes set on Avani. Seeing the boy's despair almost made Avani wonder that herself, until Rachael stepped in.

"We'll take care of her, Twilight. We promise." Rachael assured him, patting him on the head, "Why don't you go with Revy and Savannah and introduce yourself to Raiden over there? Avani and I will take care of Ninena."

Twilight smiled slightly and stepped outside the doorway, allowing Rachael into the cottage followed by Avani. Night began to pace as soon as the cottage door closed, too wrapped up in worry to notice the new addition to their waiting party.

Raiden watched as Twilight slowly approached him, but was then immediately assaulted by giggling children. Almost instantly Twilight's sullen features turned to joyfulness as he was met with hugs and enthusiastic shouts of "Twi!" by both Revy and Savannah. Soon they were all busy chasing each other around the cottage and Raiden smiled, figuring that proper introductions could wait till later.

A few minutes later, Raiden noticed sparks flying off of Night's fingertips. He was just about to point this out when he felt himself rise into the air. Looking over, he saw Revy, Savannah, and Twilight rising too, along with several small animals. He then saw even the cottage was floating as well and yet Night remained on the ground still pacing furiously.

"Night calm down, you're losing control."

Night stopped his pacing and then looked in shock at the things floating around him and then lowered everything back down to the ground.

"Sorry…" Night said, his cheeks tinted pink in a blush of embarrassment. Raiden smirked.

"I realize you're nervous, but I prefer staying on the ground."

Night smiled, relaxed by Raiden's joking manner.

"I'll try to keep it in control." he said as more sparks flew off his fingertips then he frowned. "I just realized, I still don't know your name."

Raiden smiled and then extended his hand.

"My name is Raiden."

Night shook Raiden's hand.

"I'm Night."

And then a cry rang out from the cottage. Night looked toward the front door then smiled. Facing Raiden, he seemed drunk from happiness.

"I'm a father!" he yelled as he rushed inside. Raiden followed Night inside to see a bed in the main room. In the bed Ninena was laying with a bundle of cloth. Peeking out of the cloth was a baby, her heart-shaped face was framed by curly black hair and upon looking closer Raiden noticed the baby had beautiful light green eyes.

"Her name is Cyri." Ninena said as she handed Cyri to Night. Night seemed to glow as he held his daughter in his arms and then suddenly the room was filled with the sound of wind chimes as little Cyri laughed. Rachael smiled as she watched Night with Cyri and then suddenly she became serious.

"Will you watch Revy and Savannah for me? I need to look for Leon."

Ninena smiled.

"Of course we will, you know you can always count on us."

After spending some time with Night, Ninena, Twilight, and Cyri, the trio left in search of Leon.

Chapter Two

Avani stretched and gave a little yawn as she and the others walked down the road, Night's cottage a long ways behind them.

"So Rachael, do you have any idea where Leon might be?" Avani asked, but before Rachael could reply a group of men ran out to block the trio's path. A man stepped forward, his greasy brown hair pulled back into low pony tail and his clothes dirty and worn. His voice grave, he called out.

"Give us all your money and valuables and you can pass our road unharmed!"

Rachael looked disgusted by the man and his orders and instead pulled out a golden dagger that quickly grew into a sword. Rachael whispered to the blade and the sword became encased in ice. The man smirked at the sight and then pulled out a sword of his own, the silver blade gleaming in the sun. The men behind him pulled out swords as well, some of them looking like wild animals ready for blood.

"I don't think you three can handle us *little missy*." the leader spoke. Rachael's eyes thinned at being called "little missy," but she still held her sword pointed at the lead man, her face showing her willingness to fight. Avani, seeing a fight approaching, pulled out her hair ornaments, letting her long golden hair fan out behind her. A few men from the group laughed, but their laugh soon halted when the ornaments began to elongate, turning into long deadly swords, each with a half-moon curve at the end. Raiden smirked and pulled off his necklace as well. The thieves watched as his necklace stretched, the chain thickening as it grew, each end bearing a circular sun-shaped weapon that glowed red from the heat flowing through them, spiked with long curved blades.

The leader of the thieves lunged, even though it was obvious that he was afraid, and was then quickly followed by his men. At first both Avani and Raiden were frozen in shock and amazement as they watched Rachael take on the group of thieves, blocking each attack thrown at her and causing a few injures herself. Soon some of the men broke away and lunged at Avani and Raiden.

Avani lunged toward the closet man, swinging her swords with perfect aim, one blocking the attack and the other slicing through her opponent.

Raiden too was in action, swinging his chain and then hitting his adversary with the blade at the end, making his foe scream from both the heat of the blade and the cuts inflicted. When one man came too close for Raiden to hit him with a swing of his blade, Raiden caught the man's sword in the chain and attacked with the blades at the opposite end of the chain.

For fifteen minutes the battle ensued with much pain and tears on the thieves' part, then the leader called his men back and they melted into the woods with only quiet whimpers giving them away. Rachael smiled as her blade turned back into a dagger and she put it into a sheath at her leg. Raiden returned his weapon to necklace form and then put it back on and Avani's swords shrank back into hair ornaments which she used to fix her hair back into a bun.

"You two fight well, and your weapons are very interesting. Where did you get them?" Rachael asked as she observed her travel companions. Raiden answered with a bright smile.

"Thank you, we have been training since we were both old enough to hold a sword. Our Master had our weapons specifically made for us by Mana Firesword herself. Master knew we would be his pupils even before we were born, so he asked her to make them for us and she accepted, even though it was rare for her to do so."

Surprise crossed Rachael's face at the mention of Mana Firesword, but it was quickly replaced by a broad smile.

"So you think highly of Mana?"

Both Avani and Raiden nodded their heads enthusiastically.

"Well then what did you think of her daughter?" Rachael asked, grinning wider. Avani and Raiden looked at Rachael, confused, making Rachael chuckle. “Ninena is Mana Firesword and Cloud Skysong’s daughter. And just so you know, Night is the son of Valena Fairsong and Besky Woodsmith.”

Both Avani and Raiden were shocked, their eyes wide, but before any more could be said on the subject a crack sounded from Raiden’s pocket. Reaching into it, he pulled out a small bag that Rachael recognized.

“Did Night give you that?”

Raiden nodded, smiling.

“He told me that I had to have it, and that if I keep it long enough I would meet someone interesting, but the strange thing is before he said it, his eyes got all glazed over.”

Rachael smiled in understanding.

“Night can sometimes see into the future. Did he tell you what was in it?”

Raiden shook his head, confused.

“No, only that it had been destined to be mine before I was even born.”

A sudden chirping sound erupted from inside the bag and Raiden raised his head in shock and then carefully dumped the contents of the bag into his hand. A small chick rested in Raiden’s hand, its soft plumage gold, red, and orange in color, and its eyes were a soft blue. Suddenly the chick burst into a series of chirps. Raiden listened intently and then smiled.

“Alright little one, I shall name you Sola after the sun. How’s that sound to you?”

Again the chick burst into a string of chirps. Raiden nodded and placed the chick back into the bag and then placed the bag into his breast pocket, being careful as he did so.

“So what did it say, Raiden?” Avani asked, her voice full of excitement.

"She was saying she's waited a long time to meet me...wow, can you believe it? A Phoenix has chosen *me* to be its master."

Avani smiled.

"I always knew you were special, and so did Master."

Raiden blushed.

"Well so are you Avani, that's why we were both made Master's students."

Rachael looked between the two.

"Can someone tell me what I'm missing?"

Avani smiled brightly.

"Raiden can communicate with animals. He understands them and they understand him."

Raiden smirked.

"Well your power is better than mine, Avani...So Rachael, where are we going to look for Leon first?"

Rachael looked again at the two young people with her, wondering how she had ended up with such powerful people as her guides, then smiled.

"We are going to the Brigid Mountains to find Aramat. If we find him he might be able tell us were Leon is—this is his realm after all."

As the group headed toward the mountain range, Rachael amused Avani with tales of her adventures after Rena had been defeated.

The walls were cold against his back and the chains around his wrists rubbed his skin raw, causing blood to flow freely down his arms. But Leon didn't dare use his magic to heal himself—he needed every bit of it to fight Senink, but he could feel his control slipping away with each new wound he received, the pain bringing Senink forth instead of pushing him back.

The door to the room opened and in stepped Victoria followed by Draco.

"I see you're stubborn as ever brother, but don't worry we'll soon fix that." Victoria spat at Leon as she cradled her slightly swollen belly, her dark eyes shining. She pulled out a dagger, staring at the silver blade lovingly for a few moments, then she thrust it into Leon's side, causing him to scream in agony. His whole body tensed then his head slumped to his chest, his mind fully concentrating on holding in Senink. Victoria stabbed him again, this time in the arm. Leon bit his lip to hold in the scream, inadvertently drawing blood.

"Let's see how you hold up after this." Draco said as he threw a ball of purple colored magic straight at Leon. Leon bit his lip harder.

"Aww Draco darling, let's try it together." Victoria said and then both she and Draco launched their magic at Leon. Leon let out a blood-curdling scream then he passed out. His hair turned black and his skin turned red as it healed.

"It won't be long now...soon our Lord Senink will be with us again." Draco said as he and Victoria left the room.

Inside of Leon's head a battle raged and it was beginning to seem clear who would win.

Just release me and all your pain will disappear, Senink's cold voice whispered.

"I will never allow you to gain complete control, Senink. The only way that will happen is if my soul dies!"

Senink laughed.

Come now boy, just give in. I can take control right now if I wish, but it would be much easier if you would just give in...

Leon pooled the last of his energy.

"Never!" he spat as he launched his will at Senink. Senink's cruel laughed echoed again.

Is that all you have boy? Well as you wish...we do this the hard way.

Draco and Victoria heard a scream and then cold laughter along with the sound of chains breaking. Rushing up the stairs into the room where Leon was being held, they found Senink standing, looking out the window, a cruel smile on his face revealing fangs and a forked tongue.

"Ah so you are the people responsible for my release." Senink said. Both Draco and Victoria bowed.

"Welcome back, Lord Senink." they said together, amusement and happiness in their voices.

Rachael stopped climbing for a moment as a wave of cold spread down her spine, as if something was wrong.

"Are you okay, Rachael?" Avani asked when she noticed Rachael had stopped.

"...I just had this feeling like something bad happened, but never mind. Let's keep climbing."

As she continued to climb Rachael looked up to see Sola fly close to Raiden, dropping a stone and then flying away. Rachael had been surprised by how fast the young chick was growing, but Raiden had told her Sola would grow constantly for a week and then slow down to one inch per year until she reached her adult size of an eight foot wingspan. Sola was whistling a beautiful song that warmed Rachael's saddened heart when the group finally came to the cave rumored to be the home of Aramat.

Exhausted, the trio sat down, only to be quickly surrounded by wolves. Both Avani and Rachael moved to pull their weapons, but Raiden stopped them by holding up his arm, his eyes connecting with the lead. One of the wolves stepped forward, his ice blue eyes filled with hate and anger, his hackles raised.

"Why are you mortals here?" it asked in a snarl, showing its large canines. Rachael sat up and looked the wolf straight in the eyes as she responded.

"We came seeking help from Aramat, nothing more."

The wolf growled, but was silenced by the appearance of a larger wolf, who looked to his pack, giving them the silent order to leave. Sitting down, the lead wolf looked at Rachael with what could have been a smile on his face, his large golden eyes both calm and happy.

"My apologies, but a few moons ago a man came to steal my immortality. My pack has been very protective of me ever since."

Rachael nodded, noticing at the same time that rather than hearing Aramat's words, they sounded in her head. It was an odd feeling, but it didn't feel unpleasant.

"Now, as to why you're here I already know, and I am sorry to say your mate has lost the battle against Senink and has lost control of his body. But don't fear—his soul still remains buried where Senink's was once held, all you need to do is bring him to the surface."

Rachael opened her mouth to ask a question, but Aramat answered the question before she could ask.

"Yes, it is true my fellow guardian sealed Senink's soul away, but by letting his magic remain she created a loophole to her own spell. She combined both Leon and Senink's magic, which means that when placed under extreme pain, Senink could still use the magic as a rope to pull himself out and bind Leon within. Aramet made a foolish mistake, but please forgive her for she is the youngest of us guardians and I intend to fix her mistake."

Aramat then breathed out slowly through his mouth, emitting a mist that then turned into a white rope.

"Use this to bind Senink while he's unconscious. It will then bring you, him, and your companions back to me. Now you need to know where to find him."

Rachael nodded. Aramat let out a howl that made a chill run down Rachael's spine and a young man of about seventeen appeared. He had messy black hair that reached his shoulders and intense gray eyes that made Rachael feel cornered, but what stood out the most were the wolf ears sticking out of his hair and the tail that swished behind him.

"My cub is still young, but he can help you find the people you will need to stop Senink and where Senink is located." Aramat said, pride for his son apparent in his voice. Aramat's voice then got quieter and Rachael knew he was speaking only to her.

"My cub is young and I see he will meet his mate on this adventure—please make sure nothing happens to either of them. Wolves mate for life, and I do not want my son to feel the pain that comes with losing a mate. You will need love to defeat Senink, for it is the one emotion that eludes him: Before Senink can be defeated you must find the key to his heart. For now rest here tonight and leave in the morning—the mountain is unsafe at night." Aramat said as he disappeared into the shadows. Moments later howling could be heard from beyond the cave and Rachael knew the wolves were hunting. After looking with longing toward the sound of the hunting wolves, the young man stepped forward.

"My name is Moon. It is a pleasure to be able to help you."

As Moon spoke he revealed very sharp canine teeth. Rachael smiled.

"Thank you for the help. We'll rest here tonight then leave in the morning."

Moon nodded in understanding and then sat at the edge of the cave, listening to the sounds of the hunt.

Rachael woke to the sound of Moon and Avani talking quietly.

"So your mother came here to avoid a bad marriage and fell in love with Aramat?"

Moon nodded his head solemnly.

"Yes, and I came later, but my mother died while birthing me and it broke my father's heart. Wolves mate for life, and so when my mother died, so did his love."

Avani frowned at that, but then her curiosity flared again.

"Are you immortal like your father?"

Moon smiled, his white teeth shining.

"No, I will live as long as a normal human does. Though I cannot be killed by sickness, I can still die in battle."

A short while later the group was heading down the mountain. When they reached the bottom, Moon's ears perked up and excitement flowed off of him visibly.

"Wow! This is the closest I've ever been to trees! My dad never let me come down the mountain with the others."

Rachael and Avani laughed as Moon ran in and out of the trees, sniffing them and touching the branches. Raiden was smiling at his new friend's antics, but then he sensed something and grabbed Avani, pulling her close to him and out of the way as a large black cat landed right where she had been standing. The cat looked at Avani with what Avani assumed was confusion, but as suddenly as the cat appeared, a large black wolf appeared as well, attacking the cat.

A long battle ensued with many snarls, growls, and whimpers of pain, making Raiden, Avani, and Rachael flinch as the animals fought. Finally the two broke away to stare at each other and Raiden could tell a silent conversation was happening between them. The wolf's ear was torn and blood was coming from its jaw, meanwhile the cat was much the same with a large cut on its front right leg and a small cut over its left eye. The tension left each of them as whatever conversation they were having ended and then they both passed out.

The wolf reverted into Moon, pain laced upon his face, and the cat into a girl with brown hair and cat ears sticking out with a cat tail, who too looked pained. Each had wounds similar to their animal form.

"Wonder who she is and why she attacked us." Raiden stated calmly, even though his arms were still wrapped tightly around Avani, almost as if he was afraid to let her go. Circling above him, Sola gave a startled cry as both Moon and the girl jumped to their feet. Rachael was surprised by the growl that came from Moon's human mouth, along with a hiss from the girl. She was certain no normal person could make those sounds.

"Would that be them?" Moon asked as two men suddenly appeared in a clearing a little ways away.

"Yes, they have been at it for a couple hours now." the girl responded then she turned to Avani, sorrow in her eyes.

"Sorry for attacking you, I thought you were someone else. It was wrong of me to lunge without checking."

Raiden locked his metallic blue eyes onto the girl's bright green ones, his voice slightly angered as he asked,

"Who are you? And who are those men and why are they fighting?"

The girl smiled, though Raiden could tell it was pained.

"My name is Jasmine. The man with the silver hair is my brother, and as for the reason they fight, well...that would be because of me."

Raiden was about to ask a question when the older man yelled,

"You can't beat me boy!"

The young man did not answer, just kept his purple eyes trained on his opponent's hands, ready for anything. Neither of the fighters seemed to be aware of the group of people behind them.

Moon knelt into a launching position and was about to attack the old man when Jasmine placed her hand in front of him, earning a snap at it, then the two were fighting again and so did not notice when the man with purple eyes said,

"You will see why my hair is silver, old man!" He then shot a strange metallic-gray beam at the man and when it hit him he collapsed to the ground, a solid silver statue. The man with purple eyes turned and saw the others then he fell. Jasmine noticed his fall and then rushed forward, her fight with Moon completely forgotten.

"Brother, are you okay?" Jasmine said as she cradled her brother's head into her lap. Her brother nodded then grimaced in pain, that's when Jasmine noticed the statue, "You shouldn't have used that when you were so tired! You know it makes you tired at full strength, so why did you use it now?"

Jasmine's brother smiled and brushed some hair out of Jasmine's face.

"I wasn't going to last much longer, that's why." he said, then passed out. Jasmine's tail flicked and her eyes filled with tears, her cat ears drooping down in sadness. Rachael walked over and placed her hand on the man's chest, an ice blue emitting from it. Soon the man's pain-filled expression relaxed into a peaceful one and he slipped into a deep sleep.

"He should be fine now. All he needs is some rest. While we wait, why don't you tell us your story?" Rachael said in a soft voice. Jasmine looked at her brother, worry still on her face, but after a few minutes of his quiet breathing she nodded and then sat down a little ways from her brother to give him some peace.

"My brother and I are twins. Our mother died giving birth to us and our father didn't really love us. From the moment we could walk he had us doing chores for him, working as his slaves. As we grew Jazz and I learned we had some powers: I could make things into gold and Jazz could make things turn into silver. Jazz knew father would work us both to the point of death if he found out, so he made me swear not to tell. Then we began to practice in private so that one day we could leave my father and be free. But then Jazz started to receive visions of the future and one day when I was out, he had a vision in front of our father. Our father thought he could use this to make money, but when he learned Jazz had no control over them, he decided to see if I had any powers. So to save me from our father, Jazz told him of his power with silver and from that day on my brother was worked until he passed out from exhaustion. One time when he fell asleep and accidentally rubbed his hand in his hair, he turned his hair silver. Father thought to use this ability too, but no one's hair ever turned out like Jazz's..." Jasmine smiled at the memory, lost in time for a moment.

"Later when I developed my power to transform, we finally left and we have been roaming ever since, because everywhere we go someone wants something from us...like today. That man wanted me to turn into a dragon so he could claim to be the descendent of a Dragon Warrior, but as you saw his plan didn't work..."

Rachael frowned when she heard "Dragon Warrior," but then she had an idea.

"Why don't you come with us? We could use your help and we could help you as well."

Jasmine's ears pointed straight up and she smiled as she nodded.

"One thing I would like to know is why you still have those ears and tail if your magic only deals with transformations?" Raiden asked and Jasmine blushed.

"I'm not really sure. They appeared when I gained the power, and no matter what I change into, they always come back."

Raiden smiled, amused, but said no more on the subject.

"I think we should rest here for the night and then leave in the morning when everyone is well-rested." Rachael thought out loud, hopping to get the others to agree. She felt tired, and with the mention of Dragon Warriors, she was reminded of how much she missed Leon. And so when everyone nodded in agreement, she felt happy.

Chapter Three

Senink clutched at his heart and hissed in frustration.

"Are you alright my Lord?" Victoria asked as she entered the room. Senink turned from the window he was looking out of and stared straight into Victoria's eyes.

"Your brother is still fighting me even though he grows weaker by the day…yesterday my skin finally reverted from that red he made me wear to the pale white it's supposed to be, but now that stupid half-blood is stopping all my attempts at finding out what is happening in the outside world!" Senink hissed again, his forked tongue slipping between his teeth. Draco entered the room a little wary of Senink's anger, but he continued and behind him he pulled a mountain lion cub.

"Here my Lord, you know it helps keep Leon under control…"

Senink eyed the cub in detest.

"I would rather have a human…"

Draco nodded.

"In due time my Lord. As soon as you rid yourself of Leon we will storm the kingdoms and claim what is rightfully yours." Draco didn't mention that by helping Senink destroy the kingdoms he was also avenging his mother.

Senink eyed the cub then nodded and lunged.

Rachael woke up with a gasp, covered in cold sweat, and stared at the campfire, shivering at the realness of her dream.

"Senink is awful, isn't he?"

Rachael turned to see Jazz sitting against a tree. Rachael

walked over and sat next to him.

"You know of Senink?"

Jazz nodded.

"My last few visions didn't make any sense to me so I did some research. You know, I'm surprised Senink was able to gain control over Leon—from what I've read he is the strongest wielder of Senink yet."

Rachael tilted her head in confusion.

"Can you tell me what you know of Senink? Leon didn't really tell me much when it came to him."

Jazz nodded his head, understanding in his eyes.

"Every wielder of Senink so far has either been killed at birth or have killed themselves later in life for the simple reason of this: Pain is needed to keep Senink away, so as the wielder matures, soon more and more pain is needed and then they end up killing themselves. From what I have learned, every wielder of Senink can remember the lives of the past wielders, and can remember the life of Senink up to a certain point. Also, if Senink *does* gain control, he slowly kills the soul of the original wielder."

Rachael gasped, worry for her husband even stronger than before, but Jazz smiled at her.

"From what I have learned from my visions, Leon possesses a power that stops this from happening, and that is why we have not seen much of Senink even though he has control. Rachael, did you know Leon had this power?"

Rachael smiled a small smile and shook her head, feeling grateful for her husband's ability to surprise her.

"So he should be alright then? At least, until we get him to Aramat?"

Jazz nodded.

"I wish I could tell you more, but someone is blocking my visions and it seems they are blocking Senink's as well."

Rachael was about to say something when the crystal around her neck turned green and Night's voice spoke through it.

"Rachael…I know you're busy and I know finding Leon is important, but…is there any chance you could come stop by…?"

Night's voice sounded rough and tired, which made Rachael wonder what was wrong. She had never heard her friend sound so bad. Into the stone she said,

"Alright, we should be there in a couple of days."

Night's voice sounded again and this time Rachael could detect relief in it.

"Good, see you then."

Ninena was standing at the door when the group arrived at the cottage.

"Nice to see you again Raiden, Avani. And I'm sure it will be lovely getting to know you three." Ninena said, gesturing to Moon, Jazz, and Jasmine.

"Rachael, I'm glad you came. Night has been out of it since about a month after you left."

Rachael nodded and then went for the door.

"Oh wait, I should warn you, Cyri has learned to walk and she can fly a little bit."

Raiden gawked when he heard this.

"But she's only three months old!"

Ninena smiled at this.

"Well she is part Nymph. That makes her advanced."

Raiden and Ninena continued this discussion as Rachael went into the cottage, where she was immediately tackled by several small children saying "Mommy!" and "Auntie Rachael!" Looking down at

Cyri, Rachael noticed she was rather large for her age and that she had a small pair of wings which were colored light gold with silver flecks.

"Mommy, are you here to help uncle Night?" Revy asked as he pulled on Rachael's skirt. Rachael nodded and then Cyri grabbed her hand and pulled her toward a door at the back of the cottage. She knocked on the door and then turned and left to play with the others, leaving Rachael alone in front of the door.

"Come in..." a gruff voice called. Rachael opened the door and was shocked to see Night lying on a bed in the middle of the room. He seemed gravely ill. His face was an ash gray and he looked thin.

"Oh Rachael...I wasn't expecting you so soon." Night croaked. Rachael noticed that just talking made Night more tired, for as soon as he said these words he sank deeper into the pillows propping him up and worry consumed her. How had her friend's condition become so bad?

A light knock sounded and then Ninena stepped into the room.

"Night honey, you should rest. I'll tell Rachael what is happening." Ninena said as she saw Night's tiredness, but her words where lost to him however as Night was swept into a vision. Rachael stood waiting for it to pass, but after ten minutes he was still in the vision and Rachael felt a small tug at her hand and turned to find Ninena motioning for her to follow her out of the room.

"Now you see why we called you."

Still confused, Rachael asked,

"What exactly is happening?"

Ninena looked to the door that hid Night from view, worry edged across her face.

"His visions have been coming more rapidly and are lasting much longer than normal. I mean, I was used to having to wait a few minutes to continue our conversations, but the last vision lasted two whole days."

Rachael gasped. She had never heard of a vision lasting more than an hour, but Ninena still continued to speak.

"Night can't eat or sleep when these visions come, and then when he leaves the vision his throat is too sore to eat anything thicker than broth."

Rachael stared at Ninena. She had no idea what to say. She was saved though by Jazz asking,

"When did this all really start?"

Ninena sighed, the act causing her wings to flutter a little.

"...To be honest, it's been happening since the day Senink gained control over Leon."

Senink growled and threw a dagger at the wall, barely missing Victoria.

"...What's wrong my Lord?" Victoria asked and then she flinched when Senink turned and glared at her.

"That half-breed brat is still blocking me from seeing anything!"

Victoria looked puzzled.

"Who would that be, my Lord?"

Senink hissed.

"Night Fairwood, son of Besky Woodsmith and Valena Fairsong. He seems to know when I am trying to see what is happening, but he is weakening and it won't be long until he will be out of my way..." Senink said, his cruel, cold laugh filling the room.

"And how is my Dragon Warrior coming?" Senink asked, indicating to Victoria's ballooning stomach.

"Ready to arrive any day now, my Lord..." Victoria said with a slight wince.

"Good...It is a shame the child will be half Sorcerer, but at least Draco is skilled in dark magic. You may go rest now. I don't want anything happening to the future of this world."

Victoria nodded then turned to leave. If Senink had been paying attention, he may have noticed the plan forming in Victoria's eyes, and he would have been angered by what she had in mind.

Chapter Four

It had been a week since Rachael had arrived, and Night had improved greatly. Moon healed him after every vision, enabling him to eat and talk clearly. Ninena was still worried however, because he would disappear and then return carrying armloads of wood to his room and then shut the door and lock it so no one could enter.

"Night, why is it your throat is injured after every vision no matter how well I heal it before?" Moon asked as he healed Night after another vision.

"Because that is where I chose to injure myself." Night replied simply, leaving behind Moon to puzzle his words as he retreated to his room.

"He's hiding something from us." Moon grumbled as he sat down next to Jasmine.

"Oh leave him be, everyone is entitled to their secrets." Jasmine said as she placed a hand on Moon's shoulder, only to receive a growl in reply, but before a fight could break out a knock sounded at the door. Rachael went to the door and answered it, but Ninena who had come up behind her gasped.

"Victoria!" she snarled as she raised her hands and blasted a ray of magic at her. Victoria flinched, but before the ray hit her, it disappeared.

"Welcome Victoria, I have been expecting you." Night said, causing everyone to turn and face him.

"Come, I see we have things to discuss." Night said and then Victoria followed him to his room.

"I don't like this…" Ninena said as Night closed his door. Rachael nodded in agreement, but before she could say anything a scream emitted from Night's room. Rushing toward the door, both

Rachael and Ninena where surprised when Night opened the door and carried Victoria out of the room, setting her on the couch. He turned to Ninena and Rachael and said,

"She is going into labor, I believe you should help her." and then he was swept into another vision.

Draco stood before Senink's door. He was about to go in when Victoria showed up without her baby.

"What have you done?!" Draco hissed to her before she knocked on Senink's door.

"He's angry at you for leaving the way you did, and now you don't have our child?!"

For a moment Victoria's face paled, but then a gleam came to her eyes.

"My child will grow up to know love, not hate, and it will live away from this fear and horror. You may not understand now my love, but you will someday." Victoria said and then she kissed Draco on the check and went into Senink's room, leaving Draco outside to stare at her, confused.

"...So you returned without the child?" Senink's voice hissed from the darkness. Victoria was about to answer when the air was restricted from entering her throat as Senink used one hand to crush her windpipe. Stepping out of the darkness he raised Victoria off her feet and strengthened his hold.

"You shouldn't have done that!"

Victoria gasped and touched Senink's face, her magic flowing into him without him knowing, and then the light left her eyes.

"Draco!" Senink yelled as he threw Victoria's body across the room. Draco entered the room and bowed.

"Yes my Lord?"

Senink pointed to Victoria's body and Draco paled.

"Get rid of that for me and then tell the men to get ready. We are going to visit a dear friend of ours..."

"Night, I...I'm terrified..." Victoria said quietly, her hands cradled around her bulging stomach and beads of sweat forming around her brow, "Terrified that I've made a horrible mistake by helping Draco summon Senink..." She slumped down, breathing heavily, and Night reached forward to support her.

"You don't have be a slave to Senink's demands anymore," Night urged, "Stay with us, let us help you *and* your children."

Victoria grunted and smiled weakly.

"...I'm not asking for you pity...I've done too many unforgivable things, but despite all that I could never stay, because without Draco I don't think I can go on living happily, even...if he despises me for this..." Victoria gasped and closed her eyes, her breathing becoming heavier as the pains of labor began to take over. Reaching down Night scooped her up in his arms, carrying her to the door leading to the others.

"Night!" Victoria said as he reached toward the doorknob, her purple eyes staring up at him with emotion, "Please...don't let my children grow up in a world dictated by hate and fear...please..."

Night smiled back as he stared sympathetically toward the woman who had once caused him and his friends so much pain.

"I promise to raise them as if they were my own, and I'll make certain that they can live in a world free of Senink's rage."

And when you see him, please tell Leon...I'm so sorry...

Exo and Endo stared at the room around them, their small hands clutching the air above.

"Oh they are so cute!" Avani sighed as she watched the two.

"Yes, and they will grow knowing they are loved and can learn about being good." Rachael said and Ninena nodded in agreement, both thinking back to Victoria's last wishes: She had asked as she left that her children be loved and taught how good the world is, and nothing Rachael or Ninena had said could have convinced her to stay, because she knew that in order to save her children she had to leave.

Revy, Savannah, Twilight, and Cyri were huddled around the crib playing with the babies, even though they were still unsure how to react around them.

"Too bad they will never know their mother..." Night said as he entered the room leaning heavily on the nymph staff which he had extended to full length, his voice grave and his skin ashen.

"Night, what are you doing up?" Ninena said, her voice full of concern. The visions had gotten bad again and Moon couldn't do any more to help Night.

"What? I'm not allowed to see my niece and nephew?" Night said with a smile. Rachael laughed.

"Hey now, they're my niece and nephew too!"

Night laughed as he sat down in a chair, his laugh was cut off however by a vision. A knock sounded at the door and Ninena rushed to answer it. When Ninena opened the door she was pulled into an embrace.

"So how is the new mother?" a masculine voice asked. When she was released Ninena looked up to see Robin, a smirk on his face. Behind him were the rest of her friends Fura, Fifa, Dimitreith, Ashton, Seth, Skyla, and Besky, whom had all come into the cottage, congratulating Ninena.

"So where is your little tyke? I want to introduce my son." Robin said. It was then that Ninena noticed the small children clustered among the group.

"Well who are all of these cuties?" Ninena asked. Robin pulled a small boy forward who could have been his twin.

"This is my son, his name is Shadow."

Ninena blinked and Shadow's appearance changed.

"Most of the time he looks like me, but that's only because his morph powers aren't fully developed." Robin explained.

Fura nodded in agreement.

"You should have seen Robin's face when it first happened." Fura said with a chuckle.

"So where is Night?" Robin asked and Ninena pointed to the babies' room.

Ashton stepped forward after Robin and Fura left. Huddled behind his legs was a small toddler. Her hair was platinum blonde and it formed little ringlets all the way to the small of her back, and her purple eyes were staring straight at Ninena.

"Come on sweetie, it's okay, she won't hurt you. Come meet your Auntie Ninena." Ashton said to his daughter, then he looked back at Ninena, "Sorry, she's a little shy. Her name is Aura."

Ninena crouched down to Aura's height.

"Why don't you go play with the other kids? They are in that room over there."

Aura smiled at Ninena and then ran to the room.

"She's beautiful, Ashton." Ninena said as she stood up.

"She looks like her mother…" Ashton said, his voice soft.

"…Where is her mother?" Ninena asked. Ashton sighed, pain briefly filling his eyes.

"She was killed by some of Senink's troops when they came in search of Aramet." Ashton said and then he left in search of his daughter.

Ninena started after him when she felt her leg jerked forward in a hug.

"Sethastian, you know better than that!" Fifa said, scooping up a boy. His pale green hair was filled with light blue streaks, and his joy-filled eyes the color of a tropical sea. Sethastian was roaring with laughter in his mother's arms and Fifa laughed as well, while Dimitreith explained.

"This is Sethastian, or Setty for short. And as you can see, he is a handful, just like his mother."

Fifa disentangled one of her arms to swat Dimitreith, who just smiled then they went to see Night.

Ninena looked over to Skyla and Seth, her eyebrow raised in a silent question. Skyla laughed and pointed behind her. A petite little girl stood behind one of Skyla's legs, her hair a blazing red and her eyes a soft blue with pink flecks in them. Behind her were pink wings spotted with silver.

"This is Dawn." Skyla said as she picked Dawn up, "Aaand that little man hiding behind his dad is Dusk."

Ninena looked behind Seth to Dusk, whose hair was black just like his fathers, and his eyes were his mother's lavender.

"Skyla's family apparently has a history of twins, so when we had a pair I was the only one surprised."

Skyla giggled and nodded in agreement and then they left to see Night.

"How has my son been doing?" Besky asked as he stepped forward and followed Ninena to the room, but before she could answer Avani rushed forward.

"Ninena, Night is still in a vision."

Again Ninena started to say something, but she was cut off when Night started coughing up blood from across the room, his eyes glazed over and his face contorted in pain. From somewhere deep inside his voice rang through,

"He's coming..."

Ninena had no time to puzzle over what he meant, because the crystal around her neck glowed a dark green and Terra's voice came from it.

"Ninena, I just had a vision: Senink's on his way to your cottage, but whatever happens don't let Night fight!"

With that the crystal faded and Ninena set into action. Moving the crib, she swiped her hand over the floor where a large trap door was revealed then thrust open.

"Alright, get all the children in here," then, turning, Ninena said to Jazz, "Stay with the children, I know I can trust you to defend them."

Jazz nodded then went down and Ninena closed the door after him and it blended back into the floor seamlessly. Then she moved to the opposite wall and waved her hand and opened a secret cabinet full of weapons.

"Everyone grab a weapon and get ready!" Ninena yelled. Everyone followed the command, readying themselves for Senink's attack.

Senink stared down at the cottage and growled.

"That stupid half-breed is still blocking me...Draco!"

Draco rushed forward to Senink's side and kneeled down.

"...Yes, my Lord?"

Senink smiled slightly at the fear in Draco's voice then handed him a dagger.

"This dagger is laced with Dragon Poison. I want you to take it and while I lead the attack, sneak into the cottage and kill that filthy half-breed."

Draco accepted the dagger eagerly, his anger at Night for causing his mother's and wife's deaths the only thing on his mind. He nodded and left to join the troops. After he left, Senink looked down once again at the cottage and gave the signal for attack.

Draco crept through the cottage, aware of the fighting outside. Rachael was holding her own against Senink and the others too were doing better than Senink thought they would, so Draco knew he had little time to complete his mission.

Coming to another room he felt familiar magic being used and he heard the sound of rustling leaves. Stepping into the room he found Night, his face was ashen and there was blood running down his chin and pooling on his shirt. His sky blue eyes were clear and they stared straight at Draco, as if they were reading Draco's soul.

"So you've come to kill me?" Night wheezed. Draco shuddered, gripping the handle of the dagger tighter.

"So what if I have?"

Night laughed roughly, his eyes still on Draco. They were filled with pity and something else Draco couldn't place. Suddenly Draco couldn't take the look in Night's eyes any longer and he lunged, cutting across Night's eyes then down his check and the across his chest, landing the last blow from the top of Night's right shoulder all the way down to his knuckles.

Before he could strike again he heard a whimper and turned to see a young man, his purple eyes hard with anger and his hands filled with silver light. Draco muttered a word and disappeared in a mist of shadows, leaving the dagger behind and taking guilt with him for behind the man was a young child who had tears streaming down her face and had cried out,

"Daddy!"

Somewhere in the Brigid Mountain range a woman looked up from her charges, feeling a survivor of the old race suffering. She had felt this disturbance before from the same source many times, only

this time she could feel death approaching. She was wondering if she should help when she felt her blood running through the young one's veins. Gathering up her things and her charges, she left, hoping she would make it in time.

Cyri was curled up against her father, her small hand on his chest, feeling his heart's weak beat while in the other room the adults were talking. She was unconcerned by this however, and her only thoughts were of her father.

"We need to move out of the cottage now that Senink knows that we're here." Rachael said, banging her uninjured hand on the table in rage, her other arm resting in a sling, the wrist snapped. Ninena looked at her in shock at rage.

"You mean you don't feel it?"

Everyone looked to her eyes, asking what she was talking about. Ninena sighed, wondering why no one else could feel.

"Night put up a force field, a very powerful one that only lets in those who mean us no harm. That's why Senink left so quickly...." Tears suddenly welled in Ninena's eyes as she thought of her ill husband. "What are we going to do? None of us can heal Night..." And then Ninena started to sob. Besky walked to her and then wrapped her in his arms, tears trickling down his own face. He couldn't stand the thought of losing his son either.

Everyone in the room was down; Moon and Jasmine sat next to each other, for once not fighting, Jasmine crying into Moon's shoulder as she clung to him as if he could make everything alright. Avani was encircled in Raiden's arms, crying into his shoulder and for once Raiden allowed his love for Avani to shine through, uplifting her heart if only just a little bit. Skyla, Seth, Robin, Fura, Fifa, Dimitreith, and Rachael were huddled together, their faces filled with silent tears. Jazz stood up suddenly.

"This is all my fault...if I had acted sooner Night would be just fine." he said as tears streamed down his face and guilt seeping off of him. All at once he was crushed by a group hug and voices rose, telling him how Night would be dead without him. All of this stopped however when Cyri entered the room, as if in a trance, and an unknown voice spoke out of her mouth.

"Do not be alarmed, I am a friend who wishes to help the young man in the room behind this child, but I will not be there for a couple of days so I need you to do whatever you can to keep him alive until then." And then Cyri was herself again and she ran off to be with the other children, not knowing she had just delivered a message.

"Well the question now is how do we stall for time?" Ninena asked. Jazz stepped forward.

"I could turn him into silver for a while."

Ninena looked at him and smiled.

"Great idea."

Ninena was in the kitchen watching the children and making supper when a knock sounded at the door. Telling Twilight to watch the children, she went and answered it. The woman who stood outside of the door had long, deep blue hair and blazing green eyes.

"My name is Brawen, may I come in?"

Ninena noticed Brawen seemed exhausted and her clothes were travel worn.

"Of course you can."

Brawen stepped inside then looked over her shoulder.

"May my animals come in as well? They won't harm the little ones. In fact, they'll probably play with them."

Ninena thought for a moment.

"Of course, the children would love to play with the animals and little Cyri loves them also."

Brawen smiled and then put her hand on Ninena's shoulder.

"Sorry dear, but I need you to remove that spell so I can set to work."

Ninena nodded and then went into Night's room and undid the spell, causing Night to come back to life, his breathing shallow and his wounds once again oozing blood. Brawen frowned then called behind her shoulder.

"Dark, I'll need your help."

Ninena turned toward the door and she gasped as a small dragon entered the room.

"Oh don't worry dear, my Drugons are harmless. They will attack if they feel threatened or someone threatens me, but I don't see that happening. Now you go ahead and leave this boy to me." Brawen said as she picked up the small dragon Ninena assumed was Dark. Reaching her hand out, Ninena pet Dark and was surprised by how soft his scales were and then she left Brawen to her work.

Everyone was sitting down to dinner when Brawen came into the room and sat down at an empty seat and started eating the stew that was in front of her. When she had finished she gave her report.

"He'll be fine. I managed to heal up most of his wounds. I could not return his eyes to normal however, so they'll look a little different from now on, but overall they came out much better than I had anticipated."

Ninena sat in awe at how this woman had done something no one else could.

"How can I ever repay you?" Ninena asked, ready to give Brawen anything she wanted.

"I seek no payment for healing one of my kin. I will however ask if I can remain here for the winter. The mountains get cold during the winter and I am far too old to live in those conditions..."

"Old?" Seth interrupted, "You may not be as youthful as the rest of us here, but I'd hardly consider a healthy woman of 40 to be old."

Brawen chuckled, her radiant colored hair seeming to stand out more than before.

"I appreciate the compliment, young man, but it's only by the grace of the founders of this land that I was granted my eternally youthful appearance. Long ago before the Four Kingdoms were established, a small group of skilled Sorcerers and Sorceresses, including myself, were granted immortality. In return, we became the protectors of this land, using our power to maintain balance as time went by, thus gaining the title of the 'Ancient Ones.' That's not say we're without our share of personal troubles, however. I am known as the Protector of Drugons, and so I reside in the mountains where most are found, but despite my youth I find it harder and harder to bear the winter cold throughout the years…oh, please forgive my droning on, dears."

"Brawen, you can come live with us." Fura spoke up, "Our castle is warm all year long and we have plenty of room for you and your Drugons. It's the least we could offer you for saving Night's life."

Brawen thought for a moment.

"Ah yes, that would be wonderful. I can't however go now for Luna is too close to birthing, but after that I'll gladly take you up on your offer."

Fura nodded in understanding and then the group continued conversing about Drugons. So when Night entered the room, no one noticed until he was bowed at Brawen's feet, saying something in the Nymphen language which made Brawen blush.

"I'm old, but not that old…"

Then Night looked up and everyone gasped. His eyes now had a line of gray that marred the sky blue, but before anyone could comment Night was knocked over by Cyri as she hugged him and before he could fully recover he was surrounded by his friends and family hugging him or just staring in wonder.

Chapter Five

Ninena sighed, grateful for the silence. After Night's successful recovery most of the guests had left, leaving only Brawen, Jasmine, Jazz, Moon, Avani, Raiden, and Rachael. Crying sounded, stirring Ninena from her thoughts.

"I got it." Avani yelled as she raced to see which twin was crying. Exo and Endo were growing fast and they were healthy. The only problem was their powers had come and they were still too young to control them. Exo was always bursting into flames or lighting things on fire, and on the other hand Endo was always freezing things and sometimes putting out Exo's fires.

"Raiden, help!" Avani called. Ninena rushed to see what was wrong and then paused at the doorway to laugh. Avani was holding Endo and she was frozen from the waist down. Night on the other side of the room was holding Exo and laughing hard, his eyes a shocking shade of green, but when Ninena entered the room his eyes returned to normal and he put Exo down and then left the room, unfreezing Avani as he went.

"He's been a little moody lately hasn't he?" Avani asked as she took off after Night to thank him for unfreezing her.

"She's right you know, something is different about him." Moon said as he entered the room and picked up Endo. Ninena just sat waiting for an explanation.

"He's more clumsy," Moon explained, "and every now and then his eyes turn green, I'm not sure why though."

Ninena thought about it and realized Moon was right, but before she could say anything about it a loud scream sounded from outside. Rushing out Ninena saw Night laying on the ground knocked out cold, and Avani was nowhere to be seen.

The dark room did not hide the sight of the blood spattered walls or the smell of human matter. Avani shuddered at the sight, her thoughts going out to those trapped in the room before her and of the others, hopefully safe at the cottage. As all of the despair threatened to overcome her, Avani felt a presence in the room, followed by the appearance of a soft light. Looking up from the floor, Avani saw a man leaning against the wall, his blond hair spilling into his light blue eyes and a soft gentle smile on his face.

"Who are you and how did you get in here?" Avani asked. The man looked at her as if seeing her for the first time.

"Hello Avani. I can still move around freely, just not too far from Senink. I have my mother and sister to thank for this gift, although I wish I could meet you in person."

For the first time Avani realized the light was coming from the man almost as if he was not really there, just some projected image and again she asked,

"Who are you?”

Again the man just smiled then as though he were stabbed, his face filled with pain. Avani rushed to help him, but he just stood back, the smile returning to his face.

"I don't have much time left. Know that all is well with the others and that if you pull on the ring next to the window it will open a path so you can be free. Also warn Night; tell him the Temptresses are still alive and looking for him."

As he said these words the light began to fade and so did the man's image.

"Avani, please tell Rachael I love her and that if it comes down to it, she most kill Senink...and me along with him."

With that he disappeared and Avani knew even though she had never met him before, the man who came to her aid was Leon.

Thinking of what he said Avani went to the window and pulled the ring to reveal a hidden passage. Briefly looking back at the cell, she entered the passage, the wall closing behind her.

Following the passage she found many peek holes and she spent her time looking through each of them, gradually getting the layout of the castle. Through one such hole she saw Senink. She went to turn away, but then paused when she heard him speak.

"So, Leon, still fighting me huh?"

Looking closer she saw Leon once again in his ghost-like form, leaning against a wall.

"Yes, even though you have my body does not mean I won't fight."

Senink smirked then raised his fist and squeezed it. Leon bent over in pain, gasping and clutching his side. Avani gasped as she saw blood emerge from Leon's side.

"So how do you suppose you'll stop me when the only power you have left is to create a ghost image of yourself?"

Leon breathed in deep and stood up straight, the blood gone. He then raised his hand, palm out, and let out his breath. Senink screamed as he was hurtled against the wall, small cuts appearing all over his body, but then he laughed as Leon's ghost figure sagged and coughed up blood.

"Fool, you should know you take most of the damage when this body is attacked and yet you still do it anyway. You are such a sad little weakling...you know the only way to defeat me is to do it while you are inside, but in order to do that I have to be killed and if that happens you are also killed." Senink laughed and Leon looked at the wall straight at Avani and then disappeared.

"Stupid fool still fighting me...oh well, at least this is more fun than his predecessor who just gave in. Now at least I have something to squash when I'm in need." Senink said to himself as he walked over to the window and glared out at the forest.

A knock sounded at the door.

"Lord Senink, I have something for you."

Senink opened the door and Draco walked in, pulling a wolf behind him. Senink glared.

"What is the meaning of this?"

Draco smirked then whispered a magic word. The wolf howled in pain and then morphed into Moon, his body badly bruised and some cuts along his side.

"My, what a surprise...a lone wolf in my forest?" Senink said with a smirk. Moon stared at him and growled.

"This forest is not yours, it belongs to the green ones!"

Senink's smirk turned into an expression of twisted anger.

"The *green ones* are gone."

Moon laughed a startling noise that sounded more wolf than human, and large canines appeared in his grin.

"Oh you really think so huh? My father could tell you otherwise—In fact, so could a few of the ones who oppose you."

Senink looked scared for a moment, but it was gone before Avani had time to see it.

“So who is your father? Some crack-job Sorcerer who thinks he has the power to see more than I?"

Avani gasped at the insult made to the lord of this land, but Moon just smirked, the nature of the wolf taking over.

"Oh how you would love to know..." And with that he vanished. Senink let out a yell of frustration.

"Go and find him now!" he yelled at Draco. Avani smiled and then continued her way along the path.

Ninena was pacing. Night had entered a vision soon after Avani had gone missing and it had been about four days since then and she was worried for Night's health as well as Avani's. So when the door opened she jumped and then screamed in surprise as Avani entered.

"Where have you been?! Are you okay?" Ninena asked as the others entered the room. When Raiden saw Avani he rushed to her and then encased her in a hug, tears slipping from his face as he held her close. Avani looked over Raiden's shoulder, a smile on her face.

"I know where Senink is. I was just there-"

"It's the Lost Tower." Night said as he stood up and stretched. Avani just stared at him in shock.

"Yes it is, how did you know?"

Night just smiled and then left the room with a sigh.

"So how did you escape then?" Raiden asked. Avani smiled.

"Leon helped me. He has this power to make a ghost image of himself even while Senink has control of his body."

Rachael smiled as she picked up Revy, but seeing that smile reminded Avani of Leon's words.

"Rachael, I have some bad news...according to Leon the only way to defeat Senink is to kill his host body."

Rachael grimaced at the thought.

"That is not the only way to defeat Senink...you'll see." Night said as he came back from his room holding a staff.

"Oh yeah that reminds me Night, Leon said to tell you the Temptresses are back and they are looking for you." Avani said. Night dropped his staff in panic and then looked around the room.

"Ninena, where is Cyri?"

Ninena looked at him questioningly.

"Outside, why?"

Instead of answering, Night rushed outside, his fierce anger rolling off him in the form of magic, which was causing everything and everyone to rise. Ninena was wondering what was wrong when she heard a scream from outside that turned her blood cold and then suddenly she and the others were back on the ground and rushing outside only to see Cyri crouching next to her father.

"Daddy! Are you okay?" Cyri asked, tears on her small face. Ninena scooped up her daughter and looked around wildly.

"What happened honey?" Ninena asked her.

"I was playing with Luna when these three ladies came out of the woods...and then daddy came out and yelled at them to stay away from me and then the ladies surrounded daddy...and then they touched daddy on the chest and they left holding this green thingy."

Ninena put her daughter down and then looked to Night, his breathing shallow and he was completely covered in sweat. Seeing him in this state made something in her snap. Her vision went red from anger and then when it cleared she was holding a glistening red blade. The hilt was simple, but it felt comfortable in her hand and the way the ruby blade glistened seemed somehow familiar.

"I wonder where it came from...?" she asked, shock covering her face, but no one could answer.

The man stood in the trees just above the cottage with a snarl fixed on his face. Those stupid Temptresses ruined his target—there would be no thrill in his killing, no fight to his prey...but regardless it was his assignment to kill the "half-breed," as his boss had put it, but just before the man dropped down from his tree to kill his target and perhaps even the group of people huddled around him, *it* appeared. Just the sight of it made the man's mouth water with want.

The one his boss had referred to as Ninena held the Firesword in her hand. Even from this distance the man could see the glistening of the red blade. He could feel the draw of its power and oh how he wanted it. How she had summoned the sword of Mana the man had no idea, he just knew he wanted it.

Something a few minutes east of the man's position drew his attention. A green light was glowing through the trees. Sighing, the man moved away from his target and the sword, and proceeded toward the light.

"Give it to *me*! I'm the eldest, I should be the one to eat it." One of the women below the man bellowed.

"I told you we should go back and get the winged girl! She has the same magic as this one, and the curse remains as long as she carries it!" another yelled back.

The man snickered, a plan forming in his mind. Silently he slipped to the ground and crept toward the woman holding the green orb and then using his skill as a trained thief stole it from her hands without her noticing and then he went back to his tree. Holding the orb in his hand the man could see it was not what it first appeared to be. It was round like an orb, but it was soft, not hard, and it quivered as if cold.

In his confusion he was too late to notice the thing could move, and move it did. It seemed to jump from his hand to his chest and then it sank down inside him, just above his heart. By now the Temptresses had noticed the loss of the orb and through their strange magic detected the man's presence.

"We know you're there, give us back the orb!"

The man smirked at the words. All was going as he had planned, except for the orb going into him, but that wasn't really a problem.

"Ladies, I have a proposition for you."

Night was asleep in his bed, having settled down from his heart being taken, but still Ninena was worried. *How long could someone go without their Center of Magic*? she was thinking, when Brawen cleared her throat.

"I see *they're* still around..."

Ninena looked up from Night.

"Do you know something about those evil witches?" Ninena asked, her voice filled with rage. Brawen closed her eyes for a moment, her face a mask of sadness. When she opened her eyes again she began to speak.

"Long ago when I was still young and the Four Kingdoms were just one, there was a 'school' for those users of magic. You have to understand that back then rarely did anyone have magic within them. Magic was still so new and misunderstood that if you had magic you were either hanged or used as a weapon."

Ninena flinched along with the others as they listened to Brawen.

"A facility was created to separate those with magic from those without magic."

Ninena looked puzzled.

"How did they know who had magic and who didn't?" she asked. Brawen smiled.

"It was a primitive method, but they used Truth Stones to determine whether or not you had magic based on how bright your inner color was, their logic being that brighter colors meant people were magic users. I avoided detection, because as I explained, they thought only those with bright colors had magic and when I was tested, my color was black and I was removed from the school. My friend, Rose, however was not as lucky, her magic being of bright red. After being tested and passing, the founder tested her younger sisters, Iris and Lily, and found that they too had magic. Rose begged me to help them escape and I tried many times, but they were heavily guarded. With all the magic I could muster back then, I tried one last desperate attempt to free them: I used my magic to burn down the school, but by then I was too late. My brother, who willingly helped the school officials, had cursed them. I suppose it was an experiment gone wrong, but from that day on Rose and her sisters never changed as they grew older; they never aged. Soon afterward, people with magic had begun dying by mysterious circumstances, their magic gone, and that is when I found out the truth: My friend and her sisters had caused the deaths. Rose's curse made her and her sisters need to eat 'magic hearts' of magical beings to retain their youth and to live, otherwise they'll fade to nothing. That is when all went wrong within the kingdom. The people blamed the king for allowing the school and revolted. I had to take my friend's son from her, along with her sisters', for they carried magic. The three consulted a wise woman and they found they could supposedly break the curse from eating the heart of my brother or I, and so they have been after us and our descendants ever since."

The room was quiet as everyone thought over what Brawen had said.

"Will it?" Moon asked. Brawen turned toward him.

"Will it break the curse?" Moon clarified.

"I have no way of knowing…the one thing that contained that information was lost years ago, along with Princess Sisa." Brawen said.

"That name sounds familiar, who was she?" Rachael asked.

Brawen looked sad for a moment.

"She was Senink's wife, and one of the wisest women this land has had. There was a rumor that before she was killed she placed all of her gathered knowledge into a book and gave it to her son, but no one knows if that holds true."

Rachael gasped then pulled a small book from her pocket.

"Could this be it?" she said handing the book to Brawen, who opened the book and sifted through the pages. Brawen sat down, shocked.

"So it was true…where did you get this?"

Rachael sighed, her moment of happiness over.

"It belongs to Leon. He used Ancient Magic to find what he wanted. I had it all along, which I am grateful for since Senink would only use it against us."

Brawen read a few pages, a look of enlightenment on her face.

"It all makes sense now. I know how to save Leon and stop Senink, but first we have to go find someone."

Morno grasped his heart, a layer of sweat on his face as the "Center of Magic," as those girls had called it, shifted again in his chest. As the pain passed he jumped down from the tree.

"Why does this thing keep moving?" he yelled at the three sisters. The oldest one smirked as she flipped her red hair over her shoulder.

"How should we know?" she said and then shrieked as one of Morno's daggers hit the tree behind her.

"...I know of only one reason for it to move and that is that you are related to the true owner, or maybe the true owner controls it even now. If it's uncomfortable you should just let us eat it." she said, thinking about the mouthwatering morsel. Morno thought this over for a moment.

"Will it kill him?"

The red head nodded.

"Yes it will."

Morno nodded his head.

"Fine, you may eat it. But in return you must do as I say, in other words be my servants."

The sisters huddled for a moment then turned back around.

"We agree." The oldest said and then lunged at Morno. She thrust her hand into his chest, but then she pulled it out immediately, screaming as her skin turned black. The blackness spreading, her sisters rushed to aid her, only to be consumed by the blackness as well. Soon, all that was left of them was a pile of ashes. Morno stared at the ashes in horror.

"They should have known better."

Morno turned to the voice to see a man, his dark hair covering half of his face. On his left cheek was a scar and he had black wings with gold specs that sprouted out from behind him.

"I believe you have something that belongs to a friend of mine."

Morno jumped back and drew a dagger from his boot.

"Who are you and what did you do to them? You better tell the truth—I have never missed my target."

The man smiled.

"As to who I am, my name is Robin. As to what I've done, I have not done anything. Their greed is what cost them their lives."

Morno could tell Robin was speaking the truth, but he was still confused.

"What do you mean by their greed?"

Robin sighed then sat down next to the tree Morno had just been in and patted the ground beside him.

"Come sit and I will tell you what I know."

Chapter Six

Brawen was over with Luna, Cyri right next to her.

"Alright dear, when the little ones come, put them in that basket alright?"

Cyri nodded, her small face a tight mask of concentration. Luna made a small squeaking noise and the first of her babies came into the world. A short while later all of the babies were resting in a basket, Cyri carefully watching over them as Brawen left to the kitchen.

"So, my son, how does it feel to not have magic?" Brawen asked Night who was sitting at the table. Night smiled.

"The same way it did before I knew I had it."

Suddenly Cyri shrieked. Night jerked up to run into the other room, but crashed into the wall. Gathering himself he felt his way over to the next room.

"I guess I forgot something..."

Ninena turned to Brawen's muttering.

"What did you forget?"

Brawen sighed.

"I forgot to make sure he could still see. I guess since the dagger incident he was using his magic to fill in for his eyes."

Moon sat up from lying on the floor.

"I knew something was wrong with him."

Brawen nodded.

"Alright, let's fix this. Dark, I'll need your help."

"I have problems believing you." Morno said, his dagger raised between Robin and himself. Robin sighed and then said something Morno could not hear and then Morno couldn't move.

"Sorry, but this is the only thing I can think of to prove it to you."

Night glared at Brawen.

"I have no idea what you're talking about."

Brawen sighed.

"Okay then, how many fingers am I holding up?"

Night just got up and turned away, only to hit a wall. There was a knock on the door and Ninena left Night and Brawen to continue their fight. When Ninena opened the door she was surprised to find Robin.

"Hey I brought someone you might like to meet. Is Night around?"

Ninena opened her mouth to say yes when a yelp was heard from Night. Robin smirked.

"Guess so." he said as he walked into the room where he had heard Night. Robin erupted in laughter at what he saw. Night was pinned under Brawen and Cyri was dropping something into his eyes. As the two got off him Night sat up and crossed his arms.

"If that was all you needed I could have done it myself." Night huffed. Brawen smiled then turned to Robin.

"So, how is the kin of my brother?" Brawen said as she motioned toward the man beside Robin. The man's hair was black and cropped very short, his ice blue eyes glared at Brawen.

"Your brother sends his regards."

Brawen laughed.

"I guess I'll have to stop by and see him before I move. Come

Cyri, you can help me pack." she said as she left the room. Night stared at the stranger then walked up to him, his hand held out. The man bent over in pain as a green orb left his chest and fell into Night's hand. Night raised his hand up to his chest and then sighed in relief when the green orb entered his chest. Then he was swept into a vision.

"Come on, this is going to take a while. Let me introduce you to the others." Robin said as he dragged the man into the main room.

"Everyone, this is Morno." Robin said. Ninena looked at Morno, shocked at the similarities between him and her husband. Ninena was about to say as much when Brawen entered the room, her train of Drugons following her along with Cyri.

"Well I will be leaving now. See you later." And with that she whispered something and disappeared, leaving Cyri holding a small, silver Drugon.

"Honey, did Brawen forget to take that one? Is it okay?" Ninena asked her daughter. Cyri cradled the Drugon to her chest, a pout on her face.

"She is not an '*it*.' Her name is Star, and Brawen gave her to me."

Ninena sat puzzled.

"Oh let her keep Star, you know she will even if you tell her not to, right Cyri?" Night said from behind Ninena, a smile on his face. Cyri rushed to her father.

"Thank you daddy!" she said as she hugged him and then she left giggling. Night turned to Morno and then smirked.

"So you think you can kill me, huh? Well here's your chance."

Morno wasted no time lunging at Night, both of his daggers raised, tips pointed at Night's heart, but before he could even get within a foot of Night he was lifted into the air, his daggers thrown across the room.

"Now as you can see you are no match for me. I will however

offer to train you to use that magic you have stored inside you, if you want." Night told Morno. Morno was enraged. He raised his hand to throw the dagger hidden in his sleeve when a ray of black light emerged from his hand and flew at Night. Night raised an eyebrow as he blocked the ray with a swipe of his hand, surprised by the power behind the blow.

"So Morno, what will it be? Be trained by me, or continue to taste failure?" Night said, showing his rare evil side.

Senink howled in frustration as he felt the wave of powerful magic he knew to be Night's and then another wave which had the taste of his assassin, Morno.

"Draco!" he yelled as a wave of pain hit him. Rushing into the room Draco paused and bowed then looked to his master, his face horribly bruised.

"Yes...my Lord?"

Senink smirked as he back-handed Draco, sending him flying into the wall behind him, making him almost hit a sword hanging there. As Draco stood he coughed up some blood onto the floor that was already covered in stains.

"Draco...I need that half-blood killed, and all attempts at it so far have failed. I want you to go there and win his trust then kill him."

Draco nodded and then turned to leave.

"One second Draco."

As Draco turned, Senink hit him and sent him into the wall again, this time hitting the sword hanging on it.

"After you kill him bring me your child, and Draco...*do not* fail me again."

Draco stood then bowed and left the room. Senink smirked. He knew Draco would follow his orders or die in the process.

Draco knew Senink was watching him as he made his way through the forest, but after the tree line ended, he ran. Draco now knew what Victoria had meant: He did not want any child of his anywhere near Senink, so as he headed toward Night, a final plan formed in his mind.

Morno was sweating from every pore in his body. He hadn't had this much of a workout since he killed his parents that night long ago. Night stood next to Morno without a hint of sweat or exhaustion.

"Well after you have rested we shall cont-" Night was cut off by a vision. Morno noticed Night received visions often. The one time he had tried to attack Night during a vision, he had to stay in bed for a week healing three broken ribs. As Night had explained to Morno, his magic had a built-in defense for when he entered a vision. Night came out of his vision with a glare on his face.

"Morno, be ready for an attack." Night said and then he disappeared. Morno thought for a moment and then used his morph powers to take the appearance of Robin. He smiled at his own power. Not even Night knew of his morph abilities, so maybe he could get him when he came back. As Morno thought of a plan, a figure appeared out of the forest surrounding Night's cottage. Morno jumped back as a dagger sailed toward him and then Morno saw the figure was Draco. Draco raised another dagger.

"Robin, where is Night?!" he yelled. Morno remained still.

"Behind you, Draco." Night said as he appeared behind Draco. Draco flinched, but then turned toward Night, his hands filled with black light. Morno was amazed at the battle that took place before his eyes. Draco lifted his arms and spears of shadow pierced up through the earth, encircling Night and then immediately striking for the center. A glow of green light was emitted from the mass of shadows and they disappeared, revealing Night as he stood battle-ready, his golden Nymph Staff in hand. Then both combatants launched forward, unleashing the full force of their magic at each other.

As Morno watched the fight he realized he could never beat Night at the level he was at. Now he also knew Night had been holding back when he fought him. As the battle continued both Night and Draco's brows became covered in sweat. Suddenly, Night's attack managed to made it through Draco's defenses and hit him square in the chest. A look of shock flashed over Night's face and then it was replaced by sadness as Draco's body sagged and he fell to the ground, unmoving.

"Morno, you can return to your own appearance now." Night said, his voice soft as he stared at his deceased cousin. Morno was shocked by Night's knowledge of his power. As Morno returned to the appearance he was born with, Night started to mumble something and Draco's body burst into flames. Night looked to Morno.

"We'll continue your training later." Night said and then he passed out. Looking to where Draco's body had been, Morno was surprised to see nothing, not even ashes left behind.

Senink howled in frustration as he felt Night's magic overpower Draco's, and he was even more angered at the half-blood's use of the burial magic.

"You'll never beat them, you know that? It's only a matter of time before they come for you." Leon said as his ghost form leaned against the wall.

"Counting down the days until you die, are you? Too bad you'll never see the child growing in your wife's stomach."

Leon just shrugged his shoulders and looked away into the distance. Senink's anger flared and he threw a dagger at Leon, only to have it pass through him.

"Just you wait Leon. I'll get your friends."

Ninena sat next to Night, her hand holding his.

"Morno, I thank you for not attacking him right now." she said.

"I don't think I could kill him right now even if I wanted to. Besides, I need to know what he saw before Draco died that made him so surprised."

Night groaned and then sat up, holding his head.

"Well that is the last time I ever do that." he said as a green light enveloped his body, "Ninena, can you get Rachael to come here please?"

Ninena left the room and then came back with Rachael.

"So how far along are you?" Night asked with a raise of his eyebrow. Rachael squirmed a little bit, but in return asked,

"What are you talking about?"

Night smiled and then chuckled.

"I mean, how long until you have your baby?"

Rachael gasped and then blushed, her face a cherry red.

"...Well I am actually five and a half months along, but don't worry, I can still fight!"

Night looked at her calmly and then he did something no one expected: He laughed.

"I have no doubt that you can still fight, but that doesn't mean I'll let you leave this cottage. Sorry, but you're going to have to stay here. I know that makes you mad, but it has to be done. Too much strain on your body can injure the baby."

Rachael sighed and then smiled.

"You're right, but don't think I won't fight if a fight comes my way."

Once again Night laughed and then he left the room, Morno following him.

Chapter Seven

Avani sighed as she walked down the road following behind Raiden. After Night had found out about Rachael's pregnancy he had sent both her and Raiden to find a woman named Acacia, who Night said could help stop Senink. Acacia lived in Novac, a rather large town on the Eathair and Firair border, though Avani didn't know how large until she and Raiden had finally arrived.

Avani gasped in shock at the sheer size of the town.

"How will we find Acacia here?" she asked Raiden as they entered through the main gate. Raiden thought for a moment and then walked over to a guard next to a building.

"Sir, do you know where we can find a woman named Acacia?"

The guard turned to Raiden, a weird look on his face.

"What do you need her for?"

Raiden thought for a moment.

"That really is none of your business."

The guard sneered and then grabbed Raiden by the front of his collar.

"I say it is, now tell me!"

Raiden smirked and then snapped his fingers. A small bolt of lightning shot out from them and hit the guard in the chest, making him drop Raiden. Soon both Avani and Raiden were surrounded and then carted off to jail.

"Thanks Raiden I *really wanted* to go to jail today..." Avani said, sarcasm dripping off her voice as she clutched at the bars holding them imprisoned and keeping their powers locked away.

"Well it really wasn't his business." Raiden said as he sat next to a group rats, conversing with them. The door opened, letting in sunlight which made the rats scurry away in fright. A woman and two men entered the small jail and they walked in front of the cell Raiden and Avani were in. The two men were the guards that arrested them earlier, and the woman had long soft brown hair that reached her knees, her soul-searching blue eyes regarded Avani and Raiden. As she stepped forward she leaned down and placed a hand upon each of their heads. Her eyes glowed an eerie green and then she smiled.

"These two mean me no harm. They just wish for my help in stopping Senink and you two both know how important that is so let them out."

The guards looked reluctant and one of them stepped forward—it was the one that Raiden had zapped in the chest.

"But ma'am, that one's dangerous. He nearly killed me earlier!"

Avani chuckled at the thought. Raiden had just zapped him enough to make the guard let him go, and apparently Acacia knew that as well for she turned her anger-filled blue eyes to the man who had made his accusation.

"I'm sure if this man had wanted to kill you he would have, now let them go so I may conduct my business with them elsewhere! This jail stinks of dirty men."

The guard rushed forward and did as he was told and Acacia gestured for Avani and Raiden to follow her, which they did thankfully. Avani was surprised when Acacia led them to a small tea shop on the outskirts of town and soon they were seated at a table sipping on some of the most delicious tea Avani had ever tasted.

"So what is it I can help you with?" Acacia asked, taking a sip of her own tea. Avani opened the bag at her waist and pulled out a piece of paper Night had told her to give to Acacia.

"Here, this should explain things."

As soon as Acacia took the paper an image appeared on the surface. It was a picture of a woman, and from the resemblance between Acacia and the woman in the picture, Avani thought it was a picture of Acacia herself. Then the picture faded away and a letter appeared. Avani had no idea what the letter said, but when Acacia folded the letter and placed it in her pocket, a look of confused determination was on her face.

"Take me to this 'Night.' I wish to speak to him."

Morno was upset he still couldn't beat Night, and as of their last fight he was nursing bruised ribs and a black eye, Night having used hand to hand combat against an armed Morno. Ninena came toward the tree Morno was sitting in, not so much as hiding, but just getting away from the rest of the people in Night's cottage. A smile appeared on Ninena's face. Cyri, following her, smiled as well. From where Morno was perched in his tree, it was obvious Cyri was holding Star in her arms.

"Alright, I know you're up there Morno. Come down here."

Morno was surprised Ninena knew where he was, but he didn't move, not up for whatever Ninena had planned for him. Then a sudden shake of the tree made Morno fall to the ground. He landed gracefully on his feet before falling on his butt as he was tackled by Cyri. Looking up, he was surprised to see Ninena smiling down at him. Morno didn't understand these people—he was trying to kill one of them and yet they accepted him with open arms.

"There you are, now hold still."

Morno was about to spring away from the two when he felt Ninena's cold hand on his face and then it covered his bruised eye. Morno felt Ninena's other hand on his tender ribs, pushing down slightly, and Morno gritted his teeth in order to hold back the gasp of pain that wanted to leave his throat and show weakness. The next thing Morno knew a blinding green light appeared over his black eye and then the pain was gone. Morno blinked to see Ninena looking down at him, her smile softer than before and somehow brighter.

“There, that should do you. I’ll tell Night to be more careful next time you two spar.”

And then she turned and left, leaving behind a very confused Morno who sat with Cyri on his lap, having sat up to watch Ninena go.

“Uncle Morno, will you teach me how to walk as quietly as you do?”

Morno looked down from staring after Ninena to the face of the small child in his lap.

“Momma fixed you, so please?”

And it was then that Morno realized why these people were so nice to him even if he was trying to kill one of their own: It was because to them he was family. And that’s when Morno decided he would give up on killing Night, and instead help him in his quest to destroy Senink. Looking down at Cyri, he smiled.

“Sure little one, I’ll teach you.”

And teach he did. Morno was amazed that a child so young was able to learn so quickly, and so Morno taught Cyri all of his assassin ways, glad for once to be on the other end of the teaching circle.

Morno was watching Cyri try to make herself invisible against a tree when he felt a presence he hadn’t felt before. Above him in the trees, throwing a dagger, Morno was surprised when a fellow assassin jumped out of them.

“Senink tires of you. I have been sent to kill you and all of the people in that cottage.”

Morno knew that Cyri was only a few feet from the invisible border that guarded Night’s cottage, and so knowing it was going to get very bloody very soon, Morno braced himself and then yelled to Cyri.

“Cyri, go show your momma what I just taught you while I talk with this man. I’ll be there soon.”

And as Cyri turned and began to run to the cottage, the assassin lunged. Morno blocked him, knowing he wouldn't be able to fight at full strength for a while because of his earlier fight with Night, but determined to stop the assassin before him from hurting the small girl, he fought.

Night was working on a new staff when his daughter ran into the house, her breathing ragged and a small smile on her face.

"Papa! Look what uncle Morno taught me!" she said, smiling, and then she disappeared. Night was surprised that his daughter had disappeared, but not as surprised as he was at the fact that Morno had willingly taught her something.

"I learned lots of other things too, but Uncle Morno wanted me to show momma while he talked to the man that came out of the trees, but I wanted to show you too daddy."

And then Cyri ran off, leaving Night to wonder about who the "man from the trees" was. That's when he felt a pressure on his force field and heard a muffled scream and Night began running toward the source of the scream.

When Night reached the end of his force field, he was shocked at what he saw, and so ducked behind a bush just inside the force field to watch. A tall dark man was standing in front of Morno, who was tied to a tree, spread eagle, and several daggers were embedded into the tree around him.

"Tell me how to get through and I might convince Senink to spare you, but if not I'll just take you back right now and I can't wait to see what Senink does to you." the dark man said. Night was surprised when Morno just spit in the other's face, causing the man to throw a dagger that sunk into Morno's wrist.

"Ah look, I hit you. Well I'm sure Senink won't mind." the dark man said as Morno huffed out in pain.

"You think you're invincible, Nick...ha! You will be killed as soon as you have fulfilled your purpose." Morno snarled and then he changed into the form of a small boy that Night had never seen before and slipped out of the rope binding him. Then he changed back. Pulling the dagger from his wrist, Morno smiled a cold smile, and Night watched as Nick backed away slowly.

Then Night heard a sound he wished he hadn't heard. Cyri was running toward Morno, oblivious to the danger, and before Night could react, Nick threw a dagger toward the girl. Night panicked. He knew he could never reach his daughter in time, but he tried anyway, only to be surprised when Morno threw himself in front of the dagger meant for Cyri. It sank into his chest, but Morno didn't do anything to show his pain, just threw the dagger that was in his hand, and that dagger hit its mark, sinking into Nick's throat and killing him instantly.

Morno smirked and then fell over and clutched his chest, pain showing on his face, and that is when Night rushed forward, stopping his daughter from going any closer to her uncle.

"Honey, go tell mommy and Aunt Rachael to be ready to heal someone."

Night was thankful his daughter nodded her head and ran off to the cottage. He was unsure if the danger had passed or not, and so he rushed forward on full alert toward Morno. Night lifted Morno, leaving the dagger in his chest, unsure if he should pull it out or not, and started for the cottage, not caring that he was slowly being covered by Morno's blood. He wanted to save his cousin, if only to be able to thank him for saving his daughter.

Avani could feel the magic being used as she, Raiden, and Acacia entered the force field Night had erected around his cottage, and she was worried. From what she could tell, the magic was coming from Night, Ninena, and Rachael and so she walked a little faster, knowing both Raiden and Acacia were following her.

Avani burst into the cottage and was shocked to see Morno lying on the kitchen table, a dagger sticking out of his chest, and his breathing shallow. His blood was all over Night and the table, but the three tending to him didn't seem to care about that.

"Do we take the dagger out then heal, or heal as we pull it out?" Night asked, his hand resting on the hilt of the dagger.

"Neither of us know, Night—you've asked that already, remember?" Rachael said, her voice as panicked as Night's. Avani watched as Acacia moved toward the table, her hand glowing the same green as her eyes had earlier. Avani was surprised when Acacia pushed Night out of the way and then pulled the dagger from Morno's chest, quickly slapping her glowing hand over the hole where the dagger had been. In no time at all Morno's ragged breathing smoothed out and he slipped into a peaceful sleep.

"That's what you do, Night." Acacia said as she looked into Night's eyes, and Avani was surprised by the smile that graced Night's features as he returned Acacia's gaze.

"I take it you got my letter?"

Acacia nodded then gestured to Night's filthy clothes.

"I did, and from what I can see you're just as bad as you were before. You should probably clean yourself before we get reacquainted."

Chapter Eight

Morno was tucked away in a bedroom and the table was cleaned of his blood, as was Night, when the conversation picked up again.

"So what do I have to do with Princess Sisa?" Acacia asked, getting straight to the point.

"You know how Senink is reborn every few generations?"

Acacia nodded.

"Well so is Princess Sisa. She is reborn in order to find her lost husband and heal him of his anger and regret, but for some reason the two never seem to meet."

Acacia nodded.

"And what does this have to do with me and Senink?"

Night nodded slightly, sipping the tea in front of him and wincing slightly at how hot it was.

"As you know, Sisa was Senink's wife and so it is Senink she is reborn to heal. And as for how this applies to you, you already know. There is no point trying to hide it, because I know as well."

Acacia sighed.

"I have always wondered if Nymphs are smarter than me...they seem to be able to figure out who I am with no problem."

Night just laughed and shook his head.

"No, they are not smarter than you, just more perceptive. And even then it takes them a while to figure out who you are. The only reason I figured it out so quickly is because I'm a Halfling."

Acacia nodded, a small smile on her face.

"I have always told the races to put that foolish 'pure blood' notion behind them, but do they listen to me? *No*."

Night laughed and then picked up Cyri when she tugged on his pants.

"Well maybe they will one day."

Acacia smiled and then reached across the table to grab Cyri out of Night's lap and place her in her own.

"Now your daughter will be very strong. Just look at her: You can practically see the power radiating off her."

Night smiled at Acacia, knowing the others were having a hard time keeping up with the conversation, but before he could remark upon this he was swept into a vision. Acacia sighed and turned to Ninena.

"How often is that happening?"

Ninena was surprised by suddenly being drawn into the conversation.

"A while actually, but they have been coming more frequently since Senink rose to power again."

Acacia sighed and hugged Cyri a little tighter before setting her down.

"My husband does cause trouble when he awakens, but I shall stop him this time, I know it."

Everyone in the room was taken aback by Acacia words.

"Wait, do you mean to say you're Princess Sisa?" Moon asked as he looked up from Jasmine. Acacia laughed and shook her head.

"In a way, yes. Unlike Senink who gains control of a host's body, I am born as myself and therefore use the name given to me by my parents, and I don't gain knowledge of who I am until I reach the age of sixteen, though I do have all my powers before then. And besides, I very much dislike the name 'Sisa.' It never suited me."

Silence met Acacia's words, but soon Ninena was laughing.

"Night always mentioned you disliked that name whenever he came back from a visit with you, though I never knew it was your actual name."

Acacia nodded and then looked to Night. He was still in a vision and it clearly irritated her.

"How long do those things last?" she said, gesturing to Night, and all she received in reply was a shrug.

"It ranges anywhere from a couple of minutes to a couple of days." Ninena said and once again Acacia felt irked, and so she grabbed Night by the shoulder and poured some of her magic into him, causing him to be forced out of his vision.

"Hey, that was important..." Night said in a grumble and Acacia laughed.

"Not as important as the plan I'm sure you have for me so we can stop Senink."

Night sighed and nodded in agreement.

"We still need someone before we can even try to attack Senink, and I'm afraid that person is harder to find than you. And that vision you stopped was telling me where he was."

Acacia looked guilty for a moment before she nodded her head.

"You're looking for Lain, right?"

Night nodded.

"We need him, though I doubt he will be easy to find."

Acacia just shook her head.

"Not really, he's probably in the forest. He loves to talk with the natives and eat that stupid fruit, though why it doesn't affect him is beyond me...and don't you dare say you know why Night." Acacia said as she saw the look that crossed Night's face. "I know very well that it might have to do with his being part of the forest, but that doesn't mean I think that's why."

Night just shrugged, holding his tongue, and Avani stepped up to the table.

"Do you mean the Lost Forest?" she asked Acacia and suddenly Acacia was looking Avani over, her blues eyes searching for something.

"Yes, why?"

Avani shrugged.

"I know my way around it, that's all. And I think I know the person you are speaking of. He is living with the Nature Spirits that reside there. I can take you there if you want."

Acacia raised her eyebrow and looked Avani over again before she said anything.

"I like that idea. You and I will leave tomorrow. For now though I need rest."

Avani could tell Raiden was unhappy at being left behind by the pout that was on his face, and in truth that pout made Avani want to kiss him, but instead she swatted him on the back of the head.

"I'll be fine, Raiden. I can take care of myself you know. And besides, Acacia will be with me."

Raiden just sighed and hugged Avani tightly before going back into the cottage, and then Avani ran to catch up to Acacia.

"Are you and that boy together?" Acacia asked and Avani blushed before answering.

"No, we're not."

Acacia just nodded and looked toward their destination. In no time, Avani found herself at the edge of the Lost Forest and she could feel the peace that came from being in the forest slowly sweep over her.

"Come on, Acacia. We need to go that way if we want to avoid the Lost Tower." Avani said as she tied her hand to Acacia's. Knowing that if they split up for some reason, Acacia would become lost and fall victim to the forest.

An hour after entering the forest, Avani was happy to see a tree full of the fruit only found in the Lost Forest and so as they passed she picked a few and began to eat them, loving the flavor as the juicy fruit burst in her mouth. When she looked over she noticed Acacia staring at her.

"Oh sorry, want some? They're really good."

Acacia shook her head no, and then curiosity filled her eyes.

"How long have you been eating those?"

Avani stopped so she could think and while she did, she continued to eat the fruit.

"Since I first came to the forest at the age of five. I eat them every time I come here. I really do love them, because they taste so good. I never take any home, because it feels wrong to take them out of the forest." Avani said and then she continued walking, tugging a slightly shocked Acacia behind her. Soon Avani smiled brightly.

"We're here." she told Acacia. Avani stepped through a bush and Acacia followed and was amazed by the sight before her. The village was small, but the huts in it were built right into the trees and the people of the village were surprising too. Acacia had been expecting glowing, animal-like creatures from all of the tales she had picked up over the years, but the villagers looked just like normal humans. Though from the way they regarded her, Acacia could tell they were more surprised by her presence than she was of theirs. That was when she spotted the man she had come searching for. A grin broke across her face and she went to step forward, only to have Avani put an arm in front of her to block her from moving.

"Not yet. They haven't accepted you. It would be dangerous to move until they do."

Acacia looked at Avani and she knew Avani had read the question in her eyes, because the girl was soon answering it.

"You'll know when they move again, and yes, they have accepted me. I've been here enough that I don't bother them, but you scare them. They can tell how old you really are."

Then the residents of the village moved again and Acacia released the breath she had not noticed she had been holding. Avani led her to the man she was looking for before untying the rope.

"I'll be back in a little while. There is someone I want to visit since we are here."

And then Avani left, leaving Acacia alone with Lain. The man had not changed in the two hundred years it had been since she had last seen him. He still wore his dark red hair in a ponytail, and his silver eyes still seemed to see through her. Unlike the other residents of the village, it was obvious that he was not a native.

"Interesting friend you have, Sisa. She knows more about this forest and its people than I do, and I have been living here for hundreds of years."

Acacia sighed.

"Hello Lain, my name is Acacia now. You know, I noticed she was smart when it came to the forest, but I would have never guessed she was smarter than you, though she does eat the fruit."

Lain nodded.

"Yes, I have seen her do it. And it seems she can eat it without any side effects, where as I have to be cleansed of it every now and then in order to keep my memory."

Acacia nodded and then turned to Lain, suddenly serious.

"You know why I'm here Lain. It's time to finally put an end to Senink's rampage."

Lain looked Acacia over and then sighed.

"You know what that means, right?"

Acacia sighed.

"Yes, and I can't say I'm happy about it, but it needs to be done...no matter how much it's going to hurt."

Lain nodded.

"Alright, I'll help you, though I know it's going to be hard for me to leave this forest. I come live here every time I'm reborn. The rest of the world is just changing too much for me."

Acacia nodded. She knew the feeling, though it seemed Senink was in too much of a rage to notice that the war was over. And then curiosity finally got the best of her.

"I thought the people here would look differently, but they look like normal humans." Acacia noticed, Lain giving her a strange look before he pulled a piece of fruit out of his pocket.

"Here, eat this—don't worry, it's not the memory-erasing one. It's a fruit I found that allows you to see the people in this village as they truly are."

Acacia was about to put the fruit into her mouth when it was snatched out of her hand by Avani, and Acacia had to admit she was afraid of the girl so many years her junior when she saw the look on her face.

"Are you crazy?! You can't just eat this! You have to have permission from the elder. Do you want me to get kicked out of this village because of your foolishness? And *you*—from what I've heard you're a freeloader, and you don't have permission to eat this fruit either so hand over what you have."

Acacia flinched slightly when Avani thrust her hand out for the rest of the fruit, but when Acacia turned to look at Lain, she was shocked to see surprise on his face when she had been expecting anger. And then to her surprise, Lain pulled a little bag out of his pocket and handed it to Avani.

"That's all I have, will you answer me a question? Can *you* eat the fruit?"

Acacia was curious for the answer too now that she thought of it.

"...No, I can't." Avani said and then she left, going back the same direction she had come, and the people of the village parted before her, as if afraid of her and her anger.

"Hmm...I find that interesting." Lain said as he watched her go. Acacia wondered what he meant, but before she could ask, a small child landed in her arms. At first Acacia was shocked, but then she smiled and helped the boy onto the ground. Looking up, she found a tree branch overhead she figured the boy had been climbing when he had fallen.

In the distance she saw Avani approaching, and the small boy that had landed in Acacia's arms was running to her and then tackled her to the ground. Acacia wondered why this was when a swarm of children came out of nowhere and buzzed like bees around Avani. Turning to Lain, Acacia found him to be staring at Avani intently, as if trying to read her. This continued for some while before Avani untangled herself from the children and said goodbye before heading back to her companions.

"We should leave soon. It's almost time for Shifting, and I don't want to be in the middle of the forest when they do it."

Acacia tilted her head in question.

"What's 'Shifting?'"

Avani bit her lip for a moment, looking toward the direction she has just come from as if expecting someone to come and reprimand her, and then to Acacia's surprise an old man came walking down the trail toward Avani. Avani paled, although from what Acacia could see the man was smiling and it was not long before he stood next to Avani.

The old man stood tall and even though he was slightly slumped with age, it was hard to see it in his features. His hair was a rich brown and his eyes were a vivid green that seemed to glow with knowledge.

"The Shifting is when the forest rearranges itself so that any who have come in become lost, though that never seemed to work on your friend here." the old man said, his voice strong as he placed a hand on Avani's shoulder.

"It may not make me lose my way, but the Shifting is very disorientating to others and I don't want to waste time because my companions are sick to their stomachs." Avani said, staring up at the old man, a slight hint of anger in her voice. The old man only laughed, his laugh making Acacia feel safe in a weird way.

"Of course not, dear. It would be unfortunate if you delayed in getting rid of that nuisance living in the tower."

Avani nodded and then made to tie herself to Acacia again, only to be stopped by the man.

"Would you be a dear and get my cane from my cottage?"

Avani nodded and began to walk back to the cottage and Acacia was surprised when the man turned to Lain, a thoughtful look on his face.

"You've seen it, haven't you? The spark that marks her as one of us?"

Lain nodded at the question.

"Yes I have. And it is much brighter than most of the people's here."

The old man nodded again, a small smile on his face.

"Yes, it is, but I would expect nothing less of my granddaughter. Her father was strong as well, though why he fell in love with a human is beyond me."

Acacia gasped.

"Wait, does that mean Avani is a Nature Spirit?"

The old man smiled.

"Yes. She gained her father's full power, leaving her twin brother as a simple human. It was surprising when she first appeared here at the age of five. At first we thought she was lost, but soon we realized she had been called to the forest as all Nature Spirits are, and she is the strongest Nature Spirit I have ever seen born to a human."

Lain nodded as if he understood.

"Does she know?"

The old man flinched and then smiled sheepishly.

"No one has told her, though I'm sure she has some inkling of it. But she never asks questions, and she has never asked to eat the fruit that would allow her to see the truth for herself. Though I can see that does not stop you, wanderer."

Lain smirked.

"I was given permission in my first life, old man, as you well know."

The old man nodded.

"Yes, but not in this one."

Lain laughed.

"No, but if I remember correctly, the grant lasts through all lives, whether the person has died and been reborn, or not."

The old man grumbled, but before anything more could be said on the subject, Avani returned with the old man's cane.

"Here you go, Elder. Now I am sorry to say we really must go."

The old man nodded and then kissed Avani on the forehead, his love for his granddaughter shining through, and the trio was off.

Chapter Nine

Night lifted the staff and examined it with an intense look on his face. He whispered a few words in the Nymphen Language and the wood glowed brightly for a moment then faded back to its original cherry.

"Night, what are you doing?"

Night turned to see Morno standing in the doorway, a smile on his face. Night was thankful Morno had stopped trying to kill him. It was a weird change, but Night was thankful for it none the less.

"I'm working my art."

Morno could feel the power in the room and it was intoxicating.

"So you picked up on your father's habit?" Morno asked, and the blush on Night's face was answer enough for him.

"Yeah, I guess you could say that. I love the work and my staffs sell well, though why I don't know. I'm not as skilled as my father."

Morno had to disagree with that statement, as high as he was getting from the power that filled the room. It was as if he had been put under a spell.

"I would go so far as to say you're better, Night. I can feel the power radiating from your staffs."

Again Night blushed, but this time he laughed as well.

"If you think this is intoxicating, I want you to see something."

Before Morno could answer, Night turned to one of the walls and weaved a pattern in front of it and then the wall dissolved. The power in the room was suddenly tripled and Morno was having a hard time not drooling at it and returning to his thief-like ways and just stealing the staff that Night had revealed. It was golden and had vines twining up it from the bottom all the way to the top, which held an egg-shaped, sky blue stone resting on top of it. Picking up the staff, Night held it out for Morno to hold, but Morno did not grab the staff. He could tell it was not meant for him to hold. Night noticed his hesitation and then smiled.

"This is the Nymph Staff, the strongest staff in history." Night said as he put the staff away and then resealed the wall. After that task was done, Night moved to another side of the room and picked up a staff made of black wood and then tossed it at Morno who caught it in surprise, only to feel his magic sink into the wood.

"I made that one for you. Senink is not going to be an easy opponent, and he plans to kill us off individually when we go to battle him. I for one would feel better if you held that staff in your hands, considering your lack of skill in magic."

Morno wanted to object to what Night was saying, but before he could, Night smiled.

"You've come a long way for a man who did not know he had magic two months ago, but still you don't have enough power to fight Senink should the fight call for it, which is why we are going to train as much as possible in the next three months before the war."

Morno nodded in acceptance.

Avani was happy to see the cottage, though she hadn't expected to see Night and Morno fighting outside. The battle was intense, and the magic that flowed between the two was very powerful.

"I see Night has been training Morno. That's good. The upcoming fight is going to be a hard one, and we don't want to lose anyone." Acacia stated.

The fight between the two was broken off by a vision from Night and Morno turned to Avani, a smile of welcome on his face and that in itself surprised Avani, but what surprised her more was the way

Cyri seemed to have attached herself to Morno as soon as her father went into his vision.

"Avani, you're back!" Cyri squealed, "I can't wait to show you all the cool things Uncle Morno has shown me!"

It was then that Night came out of his vision.

"Welcome back, you're just in time."

Before anyone could ask what Night meant, a scream filled the air from the inside of the cottage.

"What, already?" Morno said, whipping his head to Night, and Night nodded.

"I hope you remember your job."

Morno snorted and then jumped on top of the roof of the cottage and sat down, his legs crossed and his hands resting on his knees, a calming look on his face.

"What's going on, Night?" Avani asked, and Night just smiled.

"We are about to have a new member of the family."

Avani gasped and rushed inside only to gasp again when she noticed Leon in the room, though it was only his ghost form.

A while later Rachael was holding a small child in her arms, Leon leaning over her, a smile on his face.

"She's beautiful, honey." Leon whispered into Rachael's ear, his image flickering.

"I wish you were really here..." Rachael said sadly as her husband's image flickered again.

"I know, don't worry. I love you and I always will love you." Leon flickered again, almost disappearing. Rachael panicked.

"Leon, don't talk like that! Our daughter needs you to live—we can beat Senink together!"

Leon smiled a soft, pained smile.

“There is only one way dear, both you and I know it.” With those words Leon bent over and placed a ghost kiss upon his daughter's head. A brief whisper of “Aster” was heard before Leon's image flickered again, completely disappearing.

Avani could feel the heart break radiating off of Rachael, but before Avani could say anything, Morno entered the room. He looked completely tired.

“Sorry, Rachael...I couldn't hold him any longer.”

Before Rachael could reply to Morno, he fell over in a faint.

“I'll take care of him. I told him to just stay on the roof until I came to get him, but *no*, the stubborn fool didn't listen to me.” Night grumbled as he and Moon pulled Morno out of the room.

Avani decided now was when she wanted to see the new baby and moving toward Rachael, she was happy that Rachael held the baby up for her to hold. Avani was astonished by the beauty of the child in her arms. The baby had silver hair and turquoise eyes that seemed to stare up at her with a hidden knowledge.

“What's her name?” Avani asked Rachael, who smiled a soft, sad smile.

“Her name is Aster. That is what Leon called her, and that is what I shall name her.”

Avani nodded and then handed Aster back to Rachael. It was then that Acacia stepped forward, determination showing clearly on her face.

“Rachael, I promise you that I will get your husband back—even if it costs me my life.

Senink hissed in frustration when he finally felt Leon's presence return. He had hoped his host was gone for good.

“It almost seems as if you're unhappy to see me, Senink.” Leon said and Senink hissed again. The boy was getting on his nerves. Never before had a host put up such a resistance to his will, and never before had his host been able to stand before him. Letting his anger out, Senink shot a black beam out the window, hitting one of the trees that surrounded his hideout.

"She's beautiful, you know..." Leon said, as if only to himself.

"Oh really? And who are you referring to? Your pathetic excuse of a wife or your vile daughter?" Senink hissed, hoping to anger Leon. He was so much easier to control if he was angry, and even though Senink would never admit it, he was tired. He had been fighting too long and the war never seemed to end, but it was worth it if it could mean revenge on the fools who had taken away his chance at happiness. That is why Senink still fought: He wanted to completely destroy the Council of Elders and he knew the one way to do that was to start a war, but Senink's hopes were dashed when Leon just laughed his insult off.

The boy was quickly becoming used to Senink's harsh tongue, and the violence that hid Senink's true feelings. Senink knew he was no saint—he had killed many, and was labeled the toughest man of the war. Armies had fled before him, and yet this boy who stood before him and fought against him was unafraid, even knowing his death would be at his friends' hands.

"No Senink, I meant your wife, or have you forgotten her?" Leon said with another laugh. Senink froze, his whole body unmoving as the pain swept through him—an old ache from the scar he no longer carried.

"...What are you talking about, simpleton? She is dead—killed by my enemies a long time ago."

Leon's face was a mask of surprise. He could feel the emotions running through Senink and he had a hard time believing they were real, but how else could he explain the look upon Senink's face or the pain he felt in his own heart as it reflected Senink's emotions? And for the first time since Senink had taken over his body and forced him to become nothing more than a ghost, Leon wondered what it was exactly that had driven Senink to become so evil, and so he did the one thing he never thought he would do: He drew upon Senink's memories.

The forest clearing was filled with sunlight and Senink smiled at his love as he helped her sit down upon the blanket spread across the forest floor Sisa smiled at Senink as she cradled her swollen belly.

"Your son is kicking me like crazy! He will grow to be a great warrior someday."

Senink smiled.

"No, my love, he will grow to be whatever he wants, but he will never be a warrior. The war is over. The fools will have to draw back soon—they can't last much longer and they know it. Soon, my love, I'll be able to hang up my sword and put this whole mess behind me, and finally be the man you deserve."

Sisa smiled at her husband.

"You have always been the man I deserved. In fact, there are times when I doubt I deserve you, my love."

Senink smiled and pulled his wife to his side, his sword laying forgotten at the edge of the blanket as he pulled the picnic basket closer.

"Let's see what we have here, shall we?"

But before the basket could be opened, a group of men lunged from the forest. Senink rushed for his sword in order to defend his wife, but as he turned it was too late. A sword was blossoming from her chest and her eyes were dulled, and something inside of Senink snapped.

Leon gasped and pulled himself away from the memory. There was so much blood and so much pain.

"That's what you get for snooping through another person's memories..." Senink said with a snarled laugh, but the venom was gone, and Leon wondered how Senink really felt.

Night gasped as he came out of a vision, and it was several minutes before he could respond to the worried faces that surrounded him.

“Senink is getting ready to make his move. We need to get to the forest as soon as possible.”

And with those words everyone was in a hurry to gather things and then a question was thrown into the air by Avani.

“Wait, what about the kids? We can't take them with us, so who stays behind?”

Everyone paused in their flurry and then Jasmine stepped forward.

“I'll stay. I won't be much help in a fight.”

Moon's ears twitched at that, a little smile on his face, which was returned by Jasmine, and suddenly everyone wanted to know what was happening between them, but there was no time and soon everyone was moving out. However, Ninena spied Moon kissing Jasmine good-bye, and knew the trip would not be without conversation.

Chapter Ten

Senink stood at the ready, a sword held loosely in his hand. As soon as he saw Night come over the hill he ordered his men to attack. But before he could enter the fray himself, he froze in his tracks as his eyes landed upon the face of the woman he loved and his best friend. But none of it made sense—he had seen them both die many years ago. His head hurt and Leon, who had been resting inside of him, ready to die, felt Senink snap and then forced himself to the front of Senink's mind.

Acacia felt the change in the battle atmosphere the moment she looked down upon the field. Many of Senink's soldiers lay wounded, having lost to the powerful group of people before them. Acacia found it odd that Senink was not yelling orders. He had always been an assertive leader and could always get his men out of tight spots, but it seemed as if he wasn't there.

Looking over to where Night and Ninena were fighting together, Acacia was astonished at the power the two had. Ninena wielded her mother's Firesword, the ruby blade glistening in the sun, and many backed away from her. Night only had a simple wooden staff and many took that for granted, but they were soon proven wrong. Night wielded the staff as if it were a sword, his magic making the staff flare to life.

Across the field Moon was in his wolf form and a pack of wolves were behind him, though where they came from Acacia had no clue. All of them were lunging and working together to take the men down. Rachael was taking on twenty men by herself. She was like a whirlwind of destruction, slicing through her enemies like they were butter. Jazz seemed to be doing well by himself too. Though he had no weapon or fangs, he was efficiently taking down his enemies.

Acacia noticed Avani and Raiden were fighting together, moving as one, which made Acacia smile, because she noticed that even though her friends were taking down the enemy, they were not killing.

Still, Acacia found it odd that Senink wasn't there, and that is when she heard Ninena scream. Whipping her head in Ninena's direction, Acacia was surprised to finally see Senink, though it wasn't the way she pictured it would be. She had assumed she would see him in the throng of battle, but instead she found herself rushing forward to where Night stood frozen, his staff skewering Senink through the gut. The look on Night's face was shock, but the look on Senink's face was peaceful. He pulled himself closer to Night, making the staff run through him some more, and Acacia watched as Senink lifted his hand, whispering something into Night's ear, and then Senink fell to the ground.

Night quickly pulled the staff from Senink's body as his hair faded from black to blonde. All around them, Senink's army disappeared in poofs of smoke and Acacia realized that the army was just a force of Senink's magic and that there had never been any real soldiers.

"What happened?!" Lain yelled as he beat Acacia to Night, but Night didn't move. He just stared down at Leon's body as Rachael pulled a silver rope from her bag and began to tie it securely around Leon. Acacia stared into Night's face. His left check had a bloody hand print on it from Senink whispering in his ear, but it seemed Night didn't notice. He was too busy staring at the body of his friend.

"...He said he was sorry and that he'll never appear again."

Silence was met with Night's words, but before anyone could truly be shocked, Rachael finished the knot and they were all transported to a cave. A large wolf appeared from deeper inside.

"I see he has been stopped, but I wonder, where is Senink? He is not in his host, nor do I feel his presence."

Avani suddenly turned to the wolf.

"Aramat! Senink told Night he would never appear again, what does that mean?"

Aramat raised his hackles and growled. Moon jerked toward his father, putting himself between his father and Leon's body.

"Father, calm down!"

Aramat only growled again.

"Move out of my way, pup. That man has many things to answer to. I will not just let him kill himself!"

Moon flinched at the command, but instead of following it like he normally would, he stayed put.

"I said *move*, pup!" Aramat's voice had a commanding tone to it—the tone of an alpha wolf. Moon flinched harder, his whole body commanding him to follow orders, but he stayed none the less.

"Calm down, father!"

Aramat looked his son over, a pride in his eyes.

"You are an alpha of alphas, my son. But now you should move."

And Moon did. Rachael was worried for her husband, but all Aramat did was breathe a silver breath over Leon's body and then he howled. Immediately, three wolves appeared, dragging a body behind them. Rachael gasped. The man they dragged behind them was handsome: He had shoulder-length black hair that seemed to be multicolored, almost as if his hair was oil. His skin was a very pale white. Beside her, Acacia gasped.

"That's Senink's body, isn't it?!"

Rachael looked at Aramat to see the wolf nodding.

"Yes. I have been waiting to restore him to his proper body. It seems the fool Sorcerers who pulled his spirit from his body in the first place had no idea what they were doing. They pulled him out when he was confused, hurt, and angry, meaning he would always be confused, hurt, and angry when he was reborn, hence his uncontrollable violence."

And then Aramat breathed on Leon again and Leon woke up, while Senink's body began to breathe.

“Isn't that right, Leon? You could feel it, couldn't you? The real Senink hidden behind the anger?”

But Leon got no chance to answer, because he was pulled into a fierce hug by Rachael. When he was able to disentangle himself however, he nodded.

“Yes. Toward the end I could feel the pain, and when I visited Senink's memory to see why he would feel that way, I was able to experience firsthand the moment Senink snapped. You are right: Those fools never gave him a chance to grieve or calm down. It's a wonder he was able to hold back so much.”

Aramat nodded his agreement, but before anyone could ask what it was the two were talking about, a groan sounded from Senink's body. Acacia leaned down and cradled Senink's head onto her lap. A small gasp left everyone as Senink opened his eyes. They weren't black—they were a clear light green. For a moment Senink seemed disorientated, but then a bright smile that shocked everyone light up his face as he looked into Acacia eyes.

“Oh Sisa, my love, I had the strangest dream.”

Acacia smiled down at Senink, but the smile wasn't as bright as his. Senink seemed to sense something was wrong with his wife and he sat up, but when he did, his already pale face paled even more.

“...It wasn't a dream?”

Aramat moved before Senink and Senink seemed to cower into Acacia.

“No, it was not a dream—it was a nightmare, but don't worry. It's over now, Lord Senink. The war has been over for generations, and the Council of Elders was disbanded long ago. You have been cleared of all your crimes. I'm sorry it took me so long to restore you to your proper body.”

Senink looked deep into Aramat's eyes and smiled.

"It's alright, old friend. I'm just happy you were able to stop me in time."

And then Senink looked over to Leon, hurt in his eyes.

"Leon, I am truly sorry for all the pain I have caused you."

Leon smiled at Senink.

"It's okay, I know you didn't want to cause any harm. Besides, now I can talk to you face to face." A grin broke over Leon's face. "And Aster can learn from her grandfather."

Senink gasped and then groaned.

"Look, I may in fact be your how-many-ever-greats grandfather, but physically I am twenty, got it kid?"

At those words Leon just laughed.

"Ha! I'm older than you, so watch who you call a kid."

Senink just smiled and Night felt relief knowing that for now everything was calm and hopefully it would stay that way for a while.

About the Authors

Tamara Leann Burrell was born on November 10, 1994 in Puyallup, Washington and is currently attending Southwestern Oregon Community College to pursue a bachelor's degree in English. Her writing career began in middle school where her love of writing inspired her to create an early version of *Watair*, which eventually transformed into the Four Kingdoms Series.

As well as novel writing, Tamara takes interest in singing, music, and poem writing. Her dream is to one day become an accomplished author, starting with her first published short stories which include four books in the Four Kingdoms Series, and a one shot novel, *Pirate Princess Nascaria* published on Lulu, with future fantasy stories and poems books on the way. More of her unpublished written works can be found on http://furamara1.deviantart.com/

Racheal Lynn Gauley became acquainted with Tamara Burrell in the winter of 2008 after moving to Oregon from her previous residence in Arizona. She was born on January 20, 1993 in Long Beach, California, but has travelled around the country her whole life, and currently lives in New York while in training in the US Navy. Despite the distance between them, she and Tamara remain extremely close friends, and continue to work together on various writing projects.

An artist at heart, but also well-versed in the ways of spelling, punctuation, and formatting, Racheal Gauley was drafted as Tamara's editor/artist of the books in the Four Kingdoms Series. Pleased with her work and dedication, Tamara promoted Racheal to co-author. More of her artwork can be found at http://keyblademaster1.deviantart.com/

Thank You for Reading!

Bonus Story: The Misadventures of Blazington IV (Part 2)

Ever since that fateful day, his life has been nothing but one misfortune after another. Days had passed since then, soon weeks, months, and before he knew it, years. Despite the opportunities that presented themselves and his chances to forget his pain and humiliation, he still had only one thing on his mind even after all this time: *revenge*.

The image of his nemesis was still burned clearly into his mind even after two and a half years...albeit not as deeply as the various scabs and scars that marred his body. With careful observation, one might infer the emotional turmoil this broken man has suffered at the hands of that beastly Nymph woman, but it took only one glance to see the cosmetic damage his appearance bears as a result. His relatively emaciated frame did little to conceal the unsightly scars that covered his torso, as well as the tattered rags that once served as his noble apparel. In his unrecognizable state, the only thing that distinguished him as a former nobleman was the gold, ruby encrusted sword that hung at his waist.

The thickly forested terrain he wandered through was as hostile as it was unfamiliar to him, but after his banishment from Watair for aiding Rena and the notorious reputation he had gained as a result, he had little options when it came to shelter. As he walked along an abandoned dirt path, he winced slightly in pain at the newest additions to his scar collection. After barely managing to escape the most infamous forest in the Four Kingdoms, a run-in with the Spirits there almost cost him his life.

The restless hours of travelling had taken their toll on him, and his body had become noticeably weakened as he dragged himself down the empty pathway. Finally he came to a stop, his mind coming to face the harsh reality of the situation he was in. His body seemed to give way as he collapsed to his knees, but not even a moment later his revival was announced with the gliding of smooth metal as he stood tall, his brilliant sword pointed toward the sun and his flaming red hair blowing in the wind.

"Through hunger, exile, hopelessness and adversity, I, Blazing Von Richards IV shall never surrender to the fates! Where the sun shines bright, I will survive, and the flames of my resolve will continue to burn!" Blazington announced, breathing heavily.

"Hehe, you're funny, mister."

Blazington jumped and dropped his sword, whipping his head in surprise to see the area around him just as barren as he'd originally surmised. He heard what sounded like a slight whimper and then jumped back again as wings of red, orange, and gold unfolded before his eyes and whipped up the air around him. To his amazement, attached to the wings was a young girl in a frilly pink dress, but he only caught a glimpse of the child before she disappeared into the thicket of tress ahead, leaving behind several bright feathers floating down around him.

Blazington remained still for a moment, staring at the forest ahead, but with no reappearance of the mysterious girl, he decided to move on. Feathers had been strewn around the ground he noticed as he bent down to retrieve his sword, but a large, reddish splatter caught his eye, along with its mushy remnants.

Berries?

His eyes thinned at the pitiful remains clearly not fit to feed an animal now, but it reminded him of what his body had been craving for quite some time: food. He extended his finger toward the juicy splatter, his stomach rumbling at the prospect of any type of nourishment, but pulled it away as he realized what he was doing and instead took hold of his sword. *I still have my pride*, he convinced himself, closing his eyes and smirking. He didn't know where to locate shelter, or where to get a meal, but he knew one thing: that girl must be able to support herself somehow, and his best bet for either of those necessities must be nearby.

Sheathing his sword, Blazington stood and began making his

way off the dirt path he had been following and into the thicket of trees where the winged girl had disappeared. After barely making it out alive through the Lost Forest he wasn't thrilled about straying into another with little more than a frightened child to follow, but soon after, the occasional glimpses of loose berries at his feet reassured him he was making the right choice.

As he ventured deeper into the woods, he could make out the faint aroma of food and Blazington licked his lips in anticipation. He quickened his pace and then began to slow to a stop at the sound of people nearby. Carefully he parted his way between two large bushes and to his surprise laid eyes on a single isolated cottage. From what he could tell it was quite small, but well-built and sounded as if it currently housed a large number of people.

The wall facing him supported a smoking stone fireplace beside a single window, but before Blazington could examine it further he heard a door open and withdrew, concealing himself in the bushes. He heard several people talking amongst each other and within moments he could make some out around the corner of the cottage. First Blazington caught a glimpse of two blonde haired kids, a boy and a girl, as they said their farewells to the people nearby before leaving and disappearing into the woods. Leaning over to his left, Blazington was able to make out the rest of the crowd. Most had begun to retreat back into the cottage while only a few stayed behind, chatting idly. He saw what looked like another couple, both with black hair and simple clothing, and as he stared blankly at the man he found himself taken back to that life changing day in Castle Rain...

Scrambling to get a better view of the man who felt so familiar, his heart nearly stopped as the man and the last few stragglers made their way into the cottage, revealing the silhouette of a blonde haired woman whose skin, what little was exposed beneath a long, flowing dress, was an unmistakable Nymph green.

Blazington fell backward through the bushes and onto the ground as if the wind had been knocked out of him as thoughts of his nemesis and the undeniable hatred toward her clouded his thoughts.

With his hopes of food and shelter long forgotten, he now only thought of exacting revenge on his unsuspecting victim, and as his hand subconsciously slid across the hilt of his sword he knew he had the means to do it.

Blazington snapped himself out of such thoughts and pulled his hand away from his sword. He was getting ahead of himself—in his last encounter a reckless attempt only resulted in failure, and furthermore he couldn't be certain that it was the same woman from before, so he once again parted the gaggle of leaves and branches before him and began observing his prey. He still couldn't see her face as she still had her back to him, but from the rhythmic swishing of a handmade broom he could tell she was sweeping the walkway. Suddenly she stopped and looked out toward the woods where the kids from earlier had departed, and Blazington had to grit his teeth and clutch the fragile branches around him to keep from assaulting her at that instant.

There was no doubt in his mind now that it was the very same woman who had defeated him in Rena's castle nearly two and a half years ago. However *this* time would be much different...This time he had the upper hand: That cursed sword she used to defeat him with last time was nowhere in sight, and accompanied with the element of surprise and no one around to hinder him meant victory was imminent! Clearly this was a gift from the gods and meant for his long-awaited redemption, and while the opportunity was present he wasted no more time seizing his chance.

Blazington blasted out of the foliage serving as his camouflage and rushed toward his target. He drew his blade and in a single motion positioned it to attack. He saw the woman turn toward him, now aware of his presence, but it was too late. He brought down his sword, fully prepared to strike her down once and for all, but completely unprepared for what he saw staring down at her face to face.

Halting his sword only inches above her shoulder, what caught his attention and left him truly stunned more than the shocked expression of the woman who stood before him was the sight of her swelled stomach, leaving Blazington as lost for words as she was. In a split second his thoughts had hurdled from one extreme to the other as the realization of his assault on a pregnant woman hit him. How could he have foreseen something as unexpected as this? As unbelievable as it was, and despite his unimaginable hatred toward this woman who had ruined his life, he knew in his heart he couldn't harm a woman carrying an innocent child...until his thoughts were completely scrambled by an incredible blow beneath his jaw that sent him flying several feet onto his back.

As his sword landed beside him on the dirt, Blazington cried out in agony, stomping his feet on the ground and covering his mouth and chin with his hands. In no time the commotion attracted the attention of those in the cottage and the surprised and confused faces of various people poured out the front door.

As Blazington scrambled upright, his jaw throbbing beneath his hands, he saw the crazed Nymph woman shouting threatening remarks and flailing her broken broom as she fought against two animalistic young teens attempting to hold her back. In the forefront of the crowd was the black haired couple from before and some others, all clearly eager to defend their domain. Then Blazington heard a loud, familiar flapping of wings and behind him spotted the child he had encountered earlier, triumphantly holding out a basket of berries as she gracefully landed on the ground.

"Mommy! I brought you some fresh berries so you can make..." She stopped and stared silently at the sight of Blazington and the imposing mob that stood outside her home.

"I don't know who you are, be it an assassin or a common thief," the black haired man said, aiming a short golden staff toward Blazington, "but I suggest you leave immediately and do not return."

Twisting his lips into a snarl, something inside Blazington snapped as he slowly removed his hands from his mouth. On top of the fact that he wasn't even recognized or acknowledged amongst his former adversaries was the grim reality that not only once, but *twice* now he had been denied his vengeance, and suffered even worse as a result! With undeniable anger and hate burning inside of him (as well as the agonizing pain and swelling below his jaw), Blazington grabbed his sword and charged in the direction of the winged girl like a mad buffalo, knocking down the child and robbing her of her catch. He raced toward the forest as quickly as he could, briefly looking back at the scene behind him, a mad look in his eyes.

"HA! You haven't seen the last of Blazingto-!"

Blazington was halted in his tracks as he collided into an unsuspecting tree, once again falling backward onto the ground and dropping his stolen berries. As quickly as he could manage in his pained state, he began crawling toward the woods, scooping up all the berries he could salvage as he made his escape. Looking back through the leaves he saw the swarm of people cluttered around the girl, their perplexed faces being left behind as he crawled deeper into the forest.

"Not today, not tomorrow..." Blazington muttered, "But someday soon I shall have my *revenge*! I will not be denied!" he swore, maniacal laughter taking hold. "You will *rue* the day you made a fool of me! *Rue* it!!! MWAHAHAHAHA!!!!"

www.ingramcontent.com/pod-product-compliance
Ingram Content Group UK Ltd.
Pitfield, Milton Keynes, MK11 3LW, UK
UKHW041929190726
13854UKWH00004B/1519